They Can't Take
Your Name

They Can't Take Your Name

Your Name

A Novel

ROBERT JUSTICE

NEW YORK

"Same in Blues," 1994 by The Estate of Langston Hughes; "Let America Be America Again," "Harlem [2]," and "Tell Me" from THE COLLECTED POEMS OF LANGSTON HUGHES by Langston Hughes, edited by Arnold Rampersad with David Roessel, Associate Editor, copyright © 1994 by the Estate of Langston Hughes. Used by permission of Alfred A. Knopf, an imprint of the Knopf Doubleday Publishing Group, a division of Penguin Random House LLC. All rights reserved.

Published in the United States by Crooked Lane Books, an imprint of The Quick Brown Fox & Company LLC.

Crooked Lane Books and its logo are trademarks of The Quick Brown Fox & Company LLC.

Library of Congress Cataloging-in-Publication data available upon request.

ISBN (hardcover): 978-1-64385-842-5
ISBN (ebook): 978-1-64385-843-2

Cover design by Kara Klontz

Printed in the United States.

www.crookedlanebooks.com

Crooked Lane Books
34 West 27th St., 10th Floor
New York, NY 10001

First Edition: December 2021

10 9 8 7 6 5 4 3 2 1

For those doing time for crimes
they did not commit;
victims of the greatest injustice
in our justice system.

PART I

DREAMS DEFERRED

THE MOTHER'S DAY MASSACRE

Langston sat, but his mind raced. It never stopped.

He hated everything about prison—the guards and the food, the monotony and the boredom. He despised the caged feeling that came from knowing that his future—his very life—was out of his control.

What he hated even more was the price his family paid for his wrongful arrest and conviction. His wife, Elizabeth, aged with each visit. She tried to smile and cheer him up, but he saw how her frown lines had grown deep over the past decade.

Then there was their daughter, Liza. As her father, he yearned to watch her ambitions become her reality, but over the years his despair has only grown as she gave up everything in pursuit of his freedom.

He hated that his freedom had become her life.

Langston clenched his teeth and pounded his bed mat with both fists, their force stopped by the concrete slab beneath.

"Elizabeth, I know I have to forgive . . . but I can't."

Fists still tight.

"That governor and detective, they have done me wrong."

His fury fueled his fight.

Stay focused.

Caged as he was, he had done his best to assist his court-appointed counsel. Langston used to send them a letter each week outlining a new theory, chapter and verse, for an appeal. Each day he rehearsed the facts and reviewed the details of his case, hoping to clear his name. Even today, with all legal options exhausted, he focused on the crime itself.

Langston remembered how he and Elizabeth used to start their days with her reading him the morning paper as they sipped their coffee. The day after the murders was no different, and he remembered their surprise and sadness as they learned about the killings at the bank.

"The chief of police says that it was 'meticulous.'" Elizabeth had said. She began to read him the *Denver Post*'s account.

While the bank was officially closed, a half-dozen or so of the bank's weekend employees were huddled in the vault counting cash when the phone rang at the guard station. It was the direct line from the loading dock, which was not unusual, even for a Sunday morning, given the bank's location in one of Denver's premier skyscrapers. Deliveries happened day and night, Mother's Day included.

Police would later surmise that the guard was overpowered at the loading dock door and forced into a trash room, where he was found, skull crushed and shot. The assailant, in possession of the dead guard's two-way radio and electronic security pass, took the elevator into the bowels of the building, where he quickly made his way through the maze of underground corridors to the control room containing the building's security system. He fired one shot into the door's lock, setting off the alarm. The disguised gunman then disabled the remaining alarms, ejected the security tapes, and placed them in his backpack.

Then, he waited.

Tears welled in Langston's eyes as he thought how he and Elizabeth had assumed that the tragedy at the bank wouldn't get any closer to them than sharing sadness with coworkers. They never imagined that it would send him here, to a solitary jail cell, for so long that he would see presidents Reagan and Bush come and go.

"Oh, my God! Langston that could have been you," Elizabeth had said while reading the article in the *Post*.

To make ends meet all those years ago, he'd worked as a weekend security guard in the building in addition to his other jobs as a maintenance man and barber. On the day of the robbery and murder, however, he wasn't at his post, having asked for and received the day off to celebrate Mother's Day with Elizabeth and Liza.

He remembered Elizabeth's silent tears as she continued to read.

It was Mack Lang's first week on the job, so when the alarm sounded, bank employees heard security supervisor Jim Taylor say, "Come with me, Mack. You need to learn how to do this stuff." Both men were found dead in the hallway outside the control room.

The final remaining guard was discovered in his seat at the guard's station, victim of another gunshot wound.

In all, the assailant fired fifteen rounds from a 9mm handgun, but no bullet casings were left behind. It is assumed that the shooter took the time to pick up each one as he progressed in the robbery.

"I worked with all of those guys," Langston remembered saying as Elizabeth paused to wipe her eyes.

"The robber just appeared, we had no warning," one of the bank employees recounted. "We were counting the money, and the next thing we knew there was a gun pointed in our faces."

The intruder appeared to be familiar with the bank's procedures and knew the timing and process for assembling cash from all the branch offices at this central location to be counted and bundled. Bank employees describe the robber as calm while he tossed them two empty duffle bags and ordered them filled with the uncounted cash on the table.

"That was really smart," said the Assistant Manager, "because that uncounted cash wasn't yet bundled with the security monitors."

After locking the bank employees in the vault, the murderer walked out with almost a half-million dollars.

The *Denver Post* was the first to coin the phrase "Mother's Day Massacre," and by Monday evening every news outlet was using the moniker as well. The city was unsettled, police were on edge, and Langston, along with all of those in Five Points, the heart of Denver's black community, prayed that the perpetrator was not one of their own.

Speculation was that it was an inside job, which is why the police showed up on Langston Brown's doorstep that Monday afternoon. The detectives took his statement as to his whereabouts over the weekend and left.

Langston remembered the relief they felt a week later when the authorities announced that they had a suspect in custody. A former police officer who had moonlighted off and on at the bank.

"I worked with him too," Langston remembered telling Elizabeth. "He was ex-military, straitlaced, crew-cut dude, but I never . . ."

Nine months later, though, the *Post*'s headline read "ACQUITTED!"

"Langston, can you believe it?" Elizabeth's disbelief had been palpable.

"Those high-priced pinstripes got him off with their bag of tricks," Langston had told her.

Langston remembered when he and the guys at the barbershop watched as newly appointed Mayor Stash went on television touting the fairness of the justice system and threw his support behind the exonerated ex-cop. He announced that he was putting Detective Slager, a decorated officer with an uncanny knack for solving crimes, on the case.

It was Slager who zeroed in on Langston, and within a month Slager had him behind bars.

His name, Langston Brown, led every newscast and became synonymous with the hideous event.

He slammed his fist down again as he remembered the most troublesome fact of his case: every witness said that the murderer was white.

THE LONELIEST MONK

"Sit back and grab your elixir of choice," said the late-night radio host. "Up next we have the one, the only, Thelonious Monk."

As "'Round Midnight" began to play, something rare happened—Eli smiled.

To him, the name Thelonious Monk sounded like "the loneliest monk," which was an apt description of himself. It was the early '90s and hip-hop was the rage, but in Eli's mind jazz gave birth to hip-hop, so he decided that he would stick with the original.

The radio sat next to the door on a waist-high cabinet. Eli hooked his hat and turned toward the small, sparsely furnished room with no couch, recliner, or living room to speak of, just a kitchenette on the right and a small dining table with two chairs on the left.

"Special night, baby," Eli said as he walked to the table and lit the single, half-burned candle. "I picked up something from our favorite place."

Eli unpacked the bag and grabbed a knife and fork from the drying rack.

Sitting down at the table, he uncorked a bottle and poured. "To us," he said, raising his glass and bowing his head in thanks.

A single tear fell onto his plate. It landed on the very edge and, for a moment, teetered like a drop of rain on the Continental Divide trying to decide if it wants to become a part of the Atlantic or the Pacific Ocean. Soon it rolled down the slight slope toward the center of the plate and came to rest on the outskirts of the mashed potatoes.

He sat back and stared across the table through tear-glazed eyes at the empty chair draped with a burnt-orange scarf. It was one of the few things he kept after her death. She was—still is—his world.

"We're close, baby. Renovations are almost finished, even begun hiring people." He took a bite of the steak.

"Our dream is coming true. The Roz. Can you believe it, baby? We open next week!"

After finishing his glass with ease, Eli picked up the bottle of wine and took a long draw. "Our dream," his voice quivered, "it's almost . . ."

"Antoinette . . . I . . . I'm trying, I know what I promised, but I'm not doin' good, baby."

Eli's appetite had vanished. He stored the leftovers in the refrigerator and switched off the radio.

"Good night, my love."

Blowing out the candle, he made his way to the center of the room, where he squatted down and grabbed a hidden latch in the floor and pulled open a portal to his world below. Descending the makeshift ladder, Eli recited his mantra, "Mind. Body. Spirit."

After locking the hatch, Eli surveyed the dimly lit room, a library of sorts, with overflowing bookshelves of all sizes forming three narrow aisles, making the most of the space. On his left was a homemade, out-of-code restroom; a heavy bag hung to his right.

Eli exhaled as if to relieve a buildup of pressure.

When Eli purchased The Roz with its adjoining storage room in the back, he was just looking for a place to lie low and lay his head at night. Discovering the hollowed-out underground hiding place left over from Prohibition days was a bonus when it came to his need to lie even lower.

Three pre-cued vinyl discs sat on a record player in the corner. Eli clicked the knob, and *Kind of Blue* dropped. As the needle settled in the groove, he remembered how he read that Miles Davis used to play with his back to the audience—a silent but unmistakable protest against the status quo of segregation.

Eli turned his attention toward his books and, reaching above his head, grabbed the top corner of one of the bookshelves. With one giant pull, he dumped the contents on the ground. After the heap settled at his feet, Eli put the shelf back in its place. He reached down into the literary mess and picked up a book with a tan cover with black lettering.

He grasped the hardback with both hands and read the words on the cover out loud, "*Black Skin, White Masks*. Frantz Fanon."

He stared at the cover as if he were looking through it and reading the words on the pages beneath.

Eli quoted from memory, "'I am black, not because of a curse, but because my skin has been able to capture all the cosmic effluvia. I am truly a drop of sun under the earth.'"

Eli returned the book to its place, and—with Miles keeping him company—he continued reviewing titles in his collection, "*The Mis-Education of the Negro* by Carter G. Woodson . . . *The Souls of Black Folk* by W. E. B. DuBois . . ." *Mind*.

As Miles faded, Eli placed the last book on the bottom shelf. The needle hit the label sticker, triggering the arm to lift and float to the edge. The next album dropped—Freddie Hubbard's *Red Clay*.

Eli stripped down to his briefs, revealing numerous tattoos including a cross adorning his chest and a West African symbol marking his left forearm; on his left ribcage, a vague, unfinished outline of ink. His body, almost like a boxer's, toned for a man a few years shy of a midlife crisis.

The whir of the jump rope echoed off the cement floor as he broke a sweat and, as Hubbard handed off the lead, moved on to push-ups, pull-ups, and squats. After a round of sit-ups, Eli turned his attention to the well-worn heavy bag in the corner. Each jab and hook took its toll until the steel beam the bag was attached to reverberated with the escaping energy. As Freddie turned the corner, Eli's arms gave out.
Body.

In the shower, Eli scrubbed. Whenever he traveled outside Five Points and rubbed shoulders with the children of Europe, he always felt like there was something that stuck to him or maybe was taken from him. It wasn't that he was against white people, but sometimes—most of the time—he felt like they were against him, almost unknowingly. So he scrubbed not so much to rid himself of something but rather to reveal that which was hidden beneath his skin.

As he turned off the water, Coltrane's *A Love Supreme* cleansed his heart and soothed his soul as he dried off and dressed for bed. He lay down on an old army cot and removed the prayer bracelet from around his wrist. Fingering each of the thirty-three knots, he prayed, "Kyrie Eleison. Kyrie Eleison. Lord, have mercy."
Spirit.

Eli drifted off, knowing full well that true rest was a long way off.

MURDERER'S DAUGHTER

The next morning, Eli woke with a jolt.

Immediately and out loud he assured himself, ". . . just a dream . . . just a dream."

He'd built this underground space with the hopes that the nightmares would stop.

They had not.

Eli forced himself to think of all that he had to accomplish before opening day—hang up the liquor license, meet with the city inspector, run by the hardware store, fix the scratches in the hardwood floors caused by the day laborers he'd hired to assemble and set up the seventeen tables—and his fear dissipated.

"C'mon . . . get up. Get movin'."

Up the ladder, after a cup of coffee, Eli closed the hatch, locking away his underground world. "All right, Netty, I'll see you tonight." Antoinette never liked it when he called her that so she'd retaliate by calling him "Little Li Li." That usually stopped him for a while.

Antoinette was older than Eli by four years. They met during her college internship at his high school, where he used to follow her at a distance, hoping to orchestrate chance encounters in the hallways of Manual High School. Her grace and poise both intrigued and intimidated him. She, on the other hand, didn't know that he existed. When her internship ended, so did the relationship he'd conjured in his head.

Eli never forgot Antoinette, and three years later when their paths crossed at a mutual friend's party, he was determined not to let her get away again. Eli asked her out on the spot. Years later she told him why she agreed to go on a date, saying, "There's a sense of inner stability that comes to a man when he begins to realize that he is, in fact, a man." When Eli let on that he didn't quite follow, she simply said, "You weren't that snot-nosed kid anymore!"

He'd always known she was the one, and—after dating for only a few months—he bought a ring. At her funeral, he told the packed church about how on the day he proposed, Antoinette shouted, "Yes!" when he sank to one knee because she didn't feel the need to hear his prepared preamble before agreeing to a lifetime together. "Matrimony was made for us and us for each other," he said at the conclusion of her eulogy.

Eli mostly missed the mundane tasks of marriage. For him, grocery shopping, washing dishes, and budget meetings were just good reasons for him to spend time with Antoinette.

Children were in the plans, but an early miscarriage had their hearts running. Eli chased the dream of a big-time score in the boxing ring while handling baggage at Stapleton Airport, and Antoinette focused her pain on rescuing other people's children as a social worker. When their hearts healed, Antoinette's sickness arrived.

Though three years had passed, Eli still hadn't accepted that she'd gone, so he talked to himself—to her.

"All right, Netty, tonight we'll have the chardonnay."

Grabbing his hat, Eli stepped out onto the sidewalk and took a moment to let the sun warm the chill that had set in his bones from another night underground. With summer coming to an end and the leaves turning yellow, he made a mental note to pick up another space heater when he went to the hardware store.

His attention shifted to the firehouse across the street as he spotted the crew chief.

"Mornin', Bear," Eli shouted.

Chief Barrinton, a kind-faced, broad-shouldered man, looked up from rolling the hose in the driveway. "What up, my brotha?" he responded.

Eli then flexed a bicep. "Keep working at it; you'll catch up one of these days."

The chief smiled, then stood up, squaring his thick shoulders in Eli's direction.

"You know, all us guys here appreciate what you're doing for us. On opening night, count on it, we'll all be there."

"Means a lot, my man, truly does. Opening night's in two weeks. I'll have it ready for ya," Eli said and nodded down the street toward the front door of The Roz. "Just make sure you bring your wives and not your girlfriends!" The chief's laugh echoed through the morning air.

The Roz was the largest building in Five Points, occupying more than half the block and towering three stories above the intersection. While he hoped someday to renovate the upper floors, which were used as single-room flats back in the day, his focus and cash allowed him to concentrate only on the first level where the club was located.

As Eli walked the length of the majestic gray-stone, three-story wedge-shaped building, he reminisced about how, during its' heyday, The Roz was the place to see and be seen. At

The Roz, Ella, Duke, Basie, and Billie took the stage as they passed through town and needed to escape the sting of segregation. It was still hard for him to believe that he, fifty years later, was now the owner of the most prominent building at the five-way intersection from which the Five Points neighborhood got its name.

Five Points provided the larger city of Denver with cheap labor and an occasional eruption of anger that resulted in a few burned-out buildings and overturned cars but only mildly threatened the status quo. Even more, it was the heart of the black community. This was where they found their doctors and dentists, churches and mortuaries, bars and barbershops. Here they were safe from that which sucked so much life from them on a daily basis. After Antoinette's death, Eli moved back because in Five Points he felt like he could breathe.

As Eli walked the long block from his home toward Welton Street, he remembered telling The Roz's former owner, "Some of us ventured beyond the boundaries of Five Points not just for work but for new frontiers in the suburbs. I learned the hard way that it wasn't worth it.

"I hope that when I fix it up and the boards come off those windows that it'll bring 'em home, even if only for a night, so they might remember again who we are."

Reaching the front door, Eli stepped back to admire the new, yellow-lettered green awning. "That should draw 'em in, Netty," he said. "That and some good wine, women, and song!"

Eli opened the door. There was a "Help Wanted" sign taped on the window. Above, a balcony overlooked the stage with an outside row of booths framing an inner semicircle of tables—not a bad seat in the house. Eli had done his best to restore the room to its former glory, especially the bar. It and the stage served as dual focal points.

Eli got to work.

As he polished the bar top with its twenty-five stools, he could almost hear the conversations that would take place, the drinks spilled, and the memories made. He stocked the bar, and when each bottle stood at attention in its assigned place, he stepped back in admiration. "Almost, baby, almost."

The next few hours flowed like Rocky Mountain river water; he almost didn't hear her come in.

"Nice place," she said, not pausing for a response. "Any chance I could get a drink?"

At first all he could make out were the curves of her silhouette, but—as his eyes adjusted—her tastefully tight jeans, brown knee-high boots, and low-cut white lace blouse came into focus. The light danced on her chestnut skin as she moved across the room.

Eli reached for a grand opening flyer and began to tell her about opening night, but she sat down before he could form the words.

Eli shifted gears. "What'll ya have?"

"Give me something with some magic in it." Eli noticed the wet, mascara-smudged tissue folded over her forefinger.

He ventured, "Hard day?"

"Hard life," she said as she adjusted the blue head wrap that hid her hair and directed attention to her face.

As Eli poured, she noticed the tattoo on the inside of his left forearm. "What's that?"

"It's a symbol from Ghana." He stretched out his arm so she could get a closer look at the bird flying forward while looking back.

"What's the significance?"

"Sometimes you can't know where you are going until you know where you've come from." Eli was going to say more but didn't know what to make of the slight frown she made with her well-formed eyebrows.

She took a sip. "Liza. My name's Liza,"

"Eli Stone," he said, not knowing why he added his last name given that she hadn't.

After a few moments of silence, Liza said, "I know where I'm coming from. Hope that means I know where I'm going."

This was the reason Eli had decided not to hire a bartender but instead to do the job himself. He'd concluded that hearing the woes of others would distract him from his own. In his experience, people will share anything with their priest and their bartender.

While Eli's experience as a boxer and baggage handler at the airport didn't prepare him for the job, his three and a half decades of pain and loss more than made up for his lack of formal training.

Eli leaned into Liza's comment, "You've been crying. Do you want to talk about it?"

He studied her silence as she pushed her tissue into her pocket and retrieved another from her purse. After folding it over her finger, Liza asked Eli a question that ultimately would serve as an invitation to which he was not ready to RSVP.

"Ever heard of Langston Brown?"

Eli, along with everyone else, knew that Langston Brown had been on death row for well over a decade for the gruesome Mother's Day Massacre.

Eli nodded.

"Well," Liza said, taking a deep breath and an even longer drink, "he's my father."

A WOMAN'S DIGNITY

Eli could see the resemblance.

During the trial, coverage was constant, and Langston Brown's mugshot was a mainstay on the evening news. He was a dark-skinned black man with strong shoulders and an even stronger jaw. Liza's father was the second person tried for the Mother's Day Massacre. The first was a white former police officer acquitted in a dramatic trial that left Five Points unsettled for weeks while the rest of Denver applauded the verdict.

When Sean Slager, a detective with a seemingly uncanny knack for solving crimes, especially crimes committed by his own people, took a crack at the case, his investigation revealed a new suspect, Langston Brown.

Eli remembered how disappointed he was to find out that a child of Africa had committed such a crime. Antoinette even remarked, "Whenever one of our own robs, murders, or commits any crime outside Five Points, we all exhale a collective sigh of shame—it sets us all back. The sins of one lead to the indictment of us all."

Eli agreed.

As Liza sat before him, Eli toggled between enjoying her company and feeling guilty for being alone with a woman who was not Antoinette. He turned away to steady himself as grief and guilt tag-teamed his heart

"How old were you when it all happened?" Eli asked, his back turned, straightening the already perfectly aligned bottles.

Throughout the trial and sentencing, Eli hadn't thought about the price Langston Brown's family had paid. The legal bills and humiliation must have been difficult enough. But if he and Antoinette felt the collective shame, how much more the family must have felt an inevitable, double dose of degradation.

"Daddy was sentenced to die during my senior year of high school," she said, putting down her empty glass. "School was a nightmare with the constant whispers of my classmates, but the teachers . . . they were the worst! But we got through it. We're surviving."

"We?"

"Me and Mom. They celebrate," she made air quotes, "forty years of marriage this year. She sure meant it when she said, 'For better or for worse.'"

Back on the job refilling her glass, Eli asked, "Hope I'm not getting too personal, but how have you coped, knowing what your father did?"

"He didn't do it!" Eli was caught off guard by the fire that filled her eyes as she clenched her fists. She tensed up as if she were ready to go another round against an all-too-familiar foe.

"My father is innocent." Each word sounded like its own sentence.

"I'm sorry, I didn't mean to—"

"I've spent the past fifteen years of my life trying to clear his . . . no, *our* name . . . and when I saw the incompetence . . .

no, the *indifference* of his lawyers, that's when I knew I had to do something. It wasn't enough to be the supportive daughter . . . no. I had to become the bulldog he deserved."

Eli let her gather her thoughts as he wiped the inside of a clean glass.

"I know his case better than anyone. They didn't convict Daddy on hard evidence; the case against him is as flimsy as a paper house in a hurricane, and I'll prove it. That's why I went to law school."

"Law school?"

"All I ever wanted to do was run off to New York, start a band, record some albums, and sing my heart out. Juilliard is where I was headed, but law school is where I've been. Graduate next year."

Eli congratulated her. Liza softened.

"Don't know how I've done it. Trying to raise my daughter, all the while being the daughter my daddy needs." Tears started down her cheeks, following the familiar lines in her makeup.

Eli handed her a cocktail napkin as his mind wandered. Antoinette never wore makeup; he loved her pure beauty.

"Nope, not married." She raised her left hand, displaying a bare ring finger.

"We were engaged when Journey came along, and then he split as fast as that fancy sports car he drives turns corners. Don't believe it when a slick dude promises you the moon."

Eli recognized her pain with a nod.

"Things are tight. Momma helps, and I'm grateful, but do you know how much it costs to keep a seven-year-old in school? I can't keep up with all the field trips and fees. Then there's my school; those student loans aren't going to pay themselves. But I have to keep going. We are so close, but I'm running out of time."

Liza stared past Eli into the mirror behind the bar.

". . . I have to do it. It's the only way."

Eli sensed the change of subject but was unsure what it signaled.

"Is that what brought you in here today?"

"I love my daughter, and I love my dad. I would do anything for them."

Liza looked him in the eyes. Eli felt read.

"I have a friend, she makes good money, sets her own hours. She says that I can work with her, keep each other safe." Liza's jaw tightened. "I never thought it would come to this, never thought I'd even consider doing such a . . . but I can't see any other way."

Eli heard what she was not saying. Antoinette had told him heartbreaking stories of single mothers she'd encountered as a social worker and the things they had to do to put food on the table. "Desperation breeds desperation," she'd say.

Eli sensed that Liza was about to pay the ultimate price to stay the course and continue the fight for her father's freedom.

"You're hired!"

"What?"

"If you like, you can start now."

Eli, worried that she might misunderstand his offer as a proposition, pointed toward the "Help Wanted" sign on the window.

"We open Friday after next, but as I said, you can start anytime. There's still a lot to get done." Eli gestured around the room with both arms.

A slow smile crept onto her face.

"I accept!"

A moment passed.

"What's the job?"

They laughed.

Another moment.

"Wait, you're not open?"

Liza looked around and realized that no one else was in the bar.

HE AIN'T HEAVY

"See you tomorrow," Liza said as she headed out the door to pick up her daughter. "I'd start working right now but Mom's playing bingo tonight. Can't be late. Again, Eli, thank you so much. You've thrown me a lifeline."

Though she was in a hurry, Liza still walked slow; the heels of her boots echoed off the hardwood floors as her jeans strolled.

After he marked a couple more items off his never-ending list of tasks and added a note to pick up the "Grand Opening" sign from the printer, Eli left the list on the bar and locked up. He peeked again at the green awning. "Another day closer, baby."

He stood for a moment and surveyed the five-point inter-section. Cars sped by, most passing through on their way to greener pastures on the outskirts of the Denver. Boarded-up storefronts separated a sprinkling of barbershops, bars, and beauty salons, making an odd sort of Morse code pattern.

"Which one will we be?" His mind began to race. "What if they don't come back home? What will we do? What if The Roz ends up mothballed again?"

The smell of barbecue interrupted his worries, and Eli joined a line of people outside Zona's. Across the street from

The Roz, Zona's was the sort of place that has no tables but plenty of customers. Zona was the matriarch of Five Points and—for as long as Eli could remember—her ribs and pig-ear sandwiches were the one constant in the neighborhood.

Eli ordered two hot links and fries and turned to see a familiar face. Shemekia Turner was the local branch president of United Bank, which owned Eli's note on The Roz and adjoining building that he called home. She was picking up dinner for her family.

"Well, Mr. Stone, looks like things are shaping up." Eli could smell the fried mac and cheese, a Zona's special, wafting from her bag. A former local and college basketball star, she towered over Eli's six feet, especially in her high heels.

"Yes, Mrs. Turner, things are coming together. Now that I've hired some help, should open right on time," Eli assured her.

She and Antoinette had been college roommates and maid of honor at each other's wedding, but Eli and Shemekia used last names to acknowledge the business nature of their current relationship.

Even though Eli had the down payment in hand, he was a high-risk loan for the bank. Shemekia was out on a limb, and the loan committee at headquarters was watching.

"Sam and I will be there cheering you on."

"The best seat in the house already has your name on it," Eli said as they parted ways, both with their grease-stained bags.

Eli sat on the curb with a handful of others, all in their own worlds. As the hot link seared his taste buds, he watched the sun set behind the high-rises of the Mile High City. On this evening, Eli took special note of one of the tallest silhouettes in the evening sky. The building looked like an old-style cash register; the locals, when giving directions, actually called it the "cash register building."

The red-stone masterpiece with its reflective glass was home to some of Denver's elite businesses. Located in the ground floor lobby was the central branch of United Bank, the city's largest bank. This was the location of the Mother's Day Massacre—the crime that had Liza's father, Langston Brown, on death row.

A few blocks to the left of the bank Eli could see the central branch of Denver's library. If he could summon the courage to venture out of Five Points, he thought, he should visit and look up some of the old articles on Langston and the murders. He also wondered if Shemekia might be able to get him some information, given that she was one of the presidents.

With his tongue now numb due to the fiery spices, Eli finished his last bite and made his way home to debrief with Antoinette.

* * *

"Well, baby, I think we've found another."

Eli was halfway through the bottle as he sat across the table from Antoinette's empty chair.

A painting hung on the wall above their seats. Eli stood, bottle in hand, to get a closer look at the Gilbert Young work titled *He Ain't Heavy*. It depicted a black man atop a wall reaching down with his muscular arm and attempting to grasp the brown hand reaching up. It was the first gift he ever gave to Antoinette, and it perfectly represented who they were together. Hiring Liza made him feel like he was still on track.

He wasn't so sure about Langston. In his heart of hearts, he thought Liza was deluded thinking that her father would someday walk free.

It wasn't that Eli thought Langston was guilty; quite the opposite, he'd concluded long ago that he was most likely an innocent man behind bars. After all, the detective responsible for Langston's arrest was someone Eli had encountered in his youth.

Detective Slager had secrets, and Eli had firsthand knowledge.

As Eli stared at the picture, he tried to ignore the inevitable truth: to help Liza was to help Langston. They were intertwined.

"I think we can help Liza, but Langston . . . he feels too heavy."

Eli blew out the candle and corked the bottle.

"Good night, my love."

He descended the ladder and closed the hatch.

Mind. Body. Spirit.

The wineglass dried next to the sink, and the candle wax cooled beneath the wick. Below, Eli tilted another bookshelf, crashing its contents to the ground.

"Fyodor Dostoevsky . . . François Mauriac . . ."

His nightly therapy session was underway.

"*Les Misérables*. Victor Hugo. 'To love or have loved, that is enough. Ask nothing further. There is no other pearl to be found in the dark folds of life.'"

Eli paused. Eli wept. Miles played.

WHAT'S IN A NAME?

"Let's get you elevated," Langston would say, even to grown men, as he leg-pumped the lever on his barber chair to avoid stooping while he cut their hair. Seats were open for the other barbers, but men waited in line for Langston. Some even stayed when their turn in his chair was over so as not to miss out on what he might say to its next occupant.

Before he was a convict, Langston cut hair, among other things, at one of Five Points' many barber shops.

The painted windows would cast shadows through the shop's shotgun floor plan with its mismatched seating on the right facing the barbers and the wall-length mirror on the left. *Jet* magazine beauties plastered the walls, while the smell of blue sanitizer deodorized the room. The television in the corner silently showed Denver Broncos games and BET even when the shop was closed. Motown provided the soundtrack through a makeshift sound system. The irregular hum of the broken sterilizer went unnoticed.

Langston was a football-statured man who led East High to three basketball championships in his younger years. He wore his usual white T-shirt, dark blue Dickies, and steel-toed boots, oil- and paint-stained from his second job as an on-call maintenance man for two dilapidated apartment buildings. His bald head reflected the rotation of the ceiling fans and the flutter of the fluorescent lights. His thick beard was as dark as the black ink used for the *Denver Post*.

"Welcome back, young man. The usual, I presume." His stature was matched only by the bass in his voice.

"So, the girls chasing you yet?" The teen blushed, turning bronze. Langston's interrogation continued, "How are your grades?"

"They're good." His mother's frown told the real truth. Langston took note.

"You know, I can tell by the size of your head that you're smart. Big brains and big biceps, now that's a lethal combination!"

The young man smiled.

"What are they teaching you over there at the high school? Anything about our people? Whattabout Malcolm, Martin, and the movement?"

He glanced at the boy's mom, who pretended she was reading a magazine while she flashed her ringless ring finger in the direction of the eligible men in the room. Langston felt for the single mothers in the neighborhood who worked all day and tried to raise their children with no help at home. "We're barely making it with the two of us," he once said to his wife. "Elizabeth, I don't know how they do it."

He understood why they brought their sons to the shop— to him.

As Langston pulled the pick through his young client's coils, he began the history lesson. "Youngblood, let me tell you something. When I was a boy in Philly, I watched as my father and uncles stopped looking for work and started finding trouble in the bottom of a bottle. I'd see 'em out on the corner but barely at home. They were good men, but then life happened to them. Hope became scarce when they unionized into a whitewashed wall that locked us out of the local steel mill."

Langston brushed and oiled his clippers.

"Ya feel me, youngblood? Life is hard out there for us." The young man listened as Langston began to cut.

"Back then, I admired Martin, but it was Malcolm I followed. Martin understood the Bible and Birmingham, but he didn't realize that he had to reread his Bible if he was gonna come up north. That's why we needed Malcolm too. Don't ever forget that. We need each other."

"When did you leave Philly?" the young man asked.

"I left as soon as I was old enough to hitch, beg, and hustle. Spent a few years in Chicago, then when work dried up, decided to keep going west. I settled down in Denver 'cuz I found a woman who settled for me!" Langston stomped his foot, and the other barbers laughed on cue.

"When you find you a good woman, make sure you love her and treat her like the queen she is. If you do, she'll ride with you through thick and thin, and let me tell you a secret," Langston lowered his voice, and the boy's mom peeked over the top of her magazine. "A good woman will be your strength, so treat her like you can't survive without her, 'cuz that's the truth anyways."

As he finished the young man's lines and applied the alcohol along the edges, Langston shifted to a soft, father-like tone.

"Listen here, my man. We need to love *us* more than we love *ourselves*. Too many of us are blind to what's going on out there where the white folk live." Langston pointed in an imaginary arc that landed outside Five Points. "All of us here in this shop, we believe in you. We all counting on you to make something of yourself so you can make us all better. Ya feel me?"

Langston once told his wife, "When they get in my chair, I want them to experience hope and history. I want to free their minds, Elizabeth. I understand them 'cuz I still remember what it was like to want to look good so you could get a job and a woman and a house and some kids."

He lowered the chair and turned it toward the mirror in one motion, putting his giant hands on the young man's shoulders.

"Son, remember this—all you got is your name."

Langston now stooped down by his ear.

"No matter how hard they try, they can't take your name."

The pep talk continued even after the boy's mom paid and they made their way toward the door.

"See ya later, youngblood. Go make a name for yourself!"

The name Langston Brown meant the love of his wife and their baby girl, Liza; it meant respect for the community and his people.

Soon after Mother's Day, all that changed.

LIZA'S HOPE

Liza's gray Toyota Corolla knew the drive all too well. Head south on I-25 for two hours, turn west, and drive for another hour, and the behemoth gray building rose out of the middle of nowhere, greeting its brokenhearted guests. Stratling Correctional Facility—home of Colorado's death row.

This afternoon she started her new job at The Roz, but this morning she visited her father. Liza made it down at least once every month, twice if it was Christmas or Thanksgiving or if Journey lost a tooth and wanted Grandpa to see.

Cows littered the pastures on either side of the highway, with tributary roads leading to small towns that all but closed before the Colorado state legislature voted to privatize the prisons. Overnight, Stratling went from a dwindling community on the verge of becoming a ghost town to a place where one could earn a living wage, raise a family, and shop at Walmart.

"All because of Wakken Corrections Corporation," said one of her law school professors.

The class on the prison-industrial complex was one of her favorites. In her thesis on the subject, she wrote, "Private prisons are an alternative world where crime is good; recidivism, a sound business plan; and prisoners, a valuable commodity. With billions of dollars up for grabs, lobbyists flooded small towns everywhere with the utopian promise of the recession-proof economy of housing prisoners for profit. The members of one town council received an email stating, 'Crime Pays!: Prisons—they don't pollute, they don't go out of business, they don't downsize.' In rural communities suffering from the outsourcing of their jobs and the increasing competitiveness of crops, livestock, and oil, the lure was and is irresistible. Today, there are dozens of private prison corporations, but Wakken was the first and remains the largest. Their market-driven approach made rehabilitation a cardinal sin and repeat offenders the holy grail. Signing a contract with Wakken was guaranteed job security for a small town mayor."

Liza received an A from her professor and was invited to present to her class. She did not disappoint.

For the first time in a long time, Liza felt the promise of hope as she drove. Just yesterday, she was on the verge of the unthinkable. "Maximum Money, Minimum Time" was the proverb her girlfriend quoted to her. "Sometimes you got to do what you don't want to do to get what you want to get."

Liza wiped the corner of her eye. She was close, but then . . . Eli. "Ha!" she said, striking the steering wheel with her palm and tap-dancing her feet on the floorboard as the cruise control kept her car on track, chewing up the miles.

Where was he from? How did he get the money to reopen The Roz? Did he have a woman?

She'd been burned at the game of love and had her cherished daughter to prove it.

Liza tried to stuff her wayward thoughts about Eli, but they fought their way back like cool air on a warm day. Despite her best efforts to distract herself, she succumbed.

Eli was easy on her eyes. "Deceptively handsome" were the words that came to mind when she left The Roz the afternoon before and picked up her daughter from her mother. Something about him made her feel. Again.

Stop! her mind screamed, embarrassed at her heart. *You have to stay focused. Daddy needs you.* Then, thinking about her daughter, *Journey needs you.*

Her mind floated back to The Roz, back to Eli. He said she could wait tables but that there may be other opportunities.

Could I sing again?

Eli's eyes were kind; though his gaze penetrated her—disarmed her—she still felt safe. He reminded her a lot of her father. They both had a deep-water calm that made her feel like everything would be OK even when she thought otherwise. Liza told herself that she wouldn't talk so much next time; she was sure that he was hiding emotion when he turned his back on her.

She chastised herself again.

What are you thinking? You're in no kinda place for a relationship.

She didn't remember turning off the highway, but with her car now headed due west, she could see Stratling's flat-roofed outline peeking above the horizon in the distance.

Liza flipped down her visor, adjusting it so she could see herself in its mirror. Her scarf-wrapped head was her signature look. She wondered if people knew that she didn't have the time to do her hair, to do anything. When this ordeal began, the corners of her eyes wrinkled only when she smiled and her twenties were still in front of her.

Tilting the visor down a few degrees, she eyed the tattoo covering her chest.

Her shoulders and low-cut blouse displayed the vibrant masterpiece: an ornate, thirteen-hour pocket watch floating like a life raft upon an indigo ocean.

It took three sittings, and she had to pay the artist in installments, but it captured what she coveted most. Time.

She'd heard that the earth's tides create friction on the ocean floor. Each day, as the tides rise and roll, this friction takes its toll, ever so slightly, on the earth's rotation. Day in and day out, as the moon holds sway over the waters, the tides slow the earth's motion, imperceptibly, lengthening the amount of time in a day. She'd read that millions of years ago, days were shorter, only twenty hours or so. But as time passed and the waves rolled, hours were added. It's just a matter of time before we'll need new clocks to accommodate the extra time.

As she eyed the thirteen-hour clock etched on her chest, she wished that she—that Langston—had more time. She prayed that time would slow down enough for her to catch up, or at least catch her breath.

As she turned into the parking lot, the shadow of Stratling's razor wire sliced her view of the sky. Soon they will strip-search Langston in preparation for their visit and again afterward. She knew that her father hated the indignity, but he loved her more.

As Liza sat in the prison's visiting room, she couldn't wait to tell him about Eli, her new job, and her plan to save his life.

SKID ROW'S SAINT

After he hung the "Grand Opening" sign that announced a new beginning for the historic building and a new way of coping for himself, Eli straightened the bottles behind the bar, ensuring they hadn't left their spots.

Liza said she'd arrive in the early afternoon after visiting Langston, so Eli jotted a few notes on his yellow pad for her. He hoped that if he prepared her well, she would train the others. He planned to start her as front of house manager and then, ultimately, if she proved as competent as he suspected she would, manager in charge of all the teams. After finishing a list of items that he wanted to cover with her, he grabbed the mop and bucket.

Items like these reminded Eli of his childhood mentor, Father Myriel. A priest, Father Myriel commanded the pulpit on Sunday mornings at St. Augustine's with a humble authority that came from cleaning the toilets of the old cathedral the night before.

Five minutes north of the church building was Larimar Street, Denver's skid row, and—thanks to Father Myriel— Eli's childhood playground.

During the 1980s there was a systematic release of the mentally ill from Denver General's mental ward, and they ended up in a cell or on the streets—namely, Larimar Street.

After the assassination attempt on President Ronald Reagan, the *Denver Post* quoted Father Myriel as saying, "President Carter signed the Mental Health Systems Act to address the problem, make that the duty we have as citizens to the most vulnerable among us. However, when Reagan trounced Carter, he discarded the program and eliminated services, leaving the mentally challenged to fend for themselves."

That's what he said to the reporter on Friday, but smart local reporters knew that the best sound bites came from his sermons, so they also attended on Sunday morning with recorders in hand, and they weren't disappointed.

That Sunday he said, "I in no way condone what happened, but is it just a coincidence that John Hinckley Jr., the man who shot President Reagan, was an untreated schizophrenic man?" Then he quoted Malcolm X, "Well, once again, it looks like the chickens have come home to roost."

His picture was above the fold on Monday morning, and the headline read "LOCAL PRIEST SAYS REAGAN PUT THE BULLET IN THE GUN THAT SHOT HIM!"

For Father Myriel, justice was his message, but mercy was his mission. Virtually every day, Sunday included, he could be found on Larimar Street. While he felt helpless when it came to national policies, he did know that he could meet the practical needs of people.

As Eli wrung out the mop, he remembered how his mentor said, "A cup of cold water, in his name. Sometimes, that's all we can do."

Myriel wasn't originally from Five Points. His congregation always loved it when he told the story of his family because it was the story of their families as well.

"My father—during the great migration of Africa's children from the South to the Promised Lands of the North—saw everyone headed to New York, Chicago, and Saint Louis, so he decided to go west. The City of Angels is where God called him, but when they ran out of money and means, they decided that God was in Denver too." The congregation always laughed.

Hearing Father Myriel refer to blacks and whites as the children of Africa and the children of Europe had its effect on Eli to the point that it became a part of his everyday language. It seemed to capture an important nuance for him that, outside of the native people of this country, everyone else came here—by force or by choice—from somewhere else.

Myriel's selfless heart was matched only by his keen intellect. This round-faced, dark-skinned man of God was as quick to quote Chaucer and Achebe as he was to offer a blessing. He also had eyes to see the potential buried in the discarded youth of the city.

Eli carried the mop and bucket of gray water up the stairs to the balcony.

He thought of how he'd watch Myriel juggle his cane and an armful of sack lunches while he was in the back of the old blue van, wearing his mentor's black porkpie hat and readying the next load.

Father Myriel called each person by name as he served the sack lunches with the austerity of a downtown maître d', calling them "sir" and "ma'am."

When Myriel shouted, "Next!" Eli would jump out and sprint to his side, completing the supply chain of sandwiches, fig bars, and hot chocolate. The hungry would laugh as Myriel snatched his hat off Eli. "My bald head's gonna fry like catfish if you don't give me that back!"

Back then, Eli didn't understand how a bald head could burn when the weather was cold, but ever since he started shaving his head bald to hide the fact that he too was losing his hair, he understood.

It was Father Myriel who introduced Eli to boxing.

Recognizing that Eli, like every young boy, needed to work out his energy—and anger—Myriel would take him to the 20th Street Gym. There he learned the rhythm of the speed bag and how to dance with the heavy bag. In the ring, Eli tested himself against the older boys from the neighborhood and discovered that he could hold his own.

"If you work hard enough, you can be the next Sugar Ray Leonard," he told young Eli. "You don't want to be like those big bruisers who spend the whole fight smashing each other. No, your career will never last if you fight that way. You want to be smooth and quick like the champ."

"We were inseparable," Eli said out loud as he poured the dirty water into the utility sink. It was hard to tell who chose whom.

He made his way back to his to-do list for the satisfaction of checking off another item; then, as he emptied the mascara-stained tissues from the trash can behind the bar, his thoughts turned to Liza. She'd said that she had some good news to share with her father.

"Even though Daddy has exhausted all his appeals and no longer has a lawyer, there's still hope," she told Eli on the phone that morning. "He still has a chance, and I can't wait to tell him how we are going to get him out of there. After all these years, we're going to bring him home!"

Eli hoped Liza was right—for Eli knew what it was like to lose a father.

DADDY AND DAUGHTER

"Billieeee!" Langston greeted his daughter.

Liza had been the songbird of the Brown household, constantly harmonizing to random TV jingles as she danced around the house. After blowing out her candles on her seventh birthday, she informed all present that she had wished for voice and piano lessons. Elizabeth picked up an extra shift at Woolworth's, and Langston added an extra day at the barbershop to make her dream come true.

"Elizabeth, she's our Billie Holiday, our own little Lady Day," they would say. Plus calling Liza "Billie" helped prevent people from confusing her with her mother, Elizabeth.

"Hi, Daddy," she said.

They hugged for a long time as he spoke into her hair just above her ear.

"Billie, you don't have to visit me so often. I love seeing you, but it doesn't make sense that you drive all this way just to sit in this cold room. Next time we can just talk by phone."

"No can do," she replied.

They sat in the faded yellow plastic chairs. His handcuffs scraped across the cold metal table as they held hands.

Langston was used to the constant gaze of the guards though their fickleness sometimes got to him. Today they decided to leave the chains on his ankles and wrists.

"Daddy, I don't know how you do it, how do you put up with them?" She shot a glare at one of the guards on the other side of the observation window.

"Oh, don't pay them no mind." Langston was undeterred. "How's my beautiful grandbaby?"

Journey had never known Langston as a free man. He first told his infant granddaughter that he loved her through the crackle of an intercom phone as he gazed upon her melanin-ready skin through the fogged glass that kept him from kissing her forehead. Seven years had passed, and because of a prison reform bill lobbied for by the NAACP, Journey and Langston could now hug and high-five whenever she visited.

"She's good, just started second grade."

"You know, Billie, if I ever get out of here, I'm going to find that sorry excuse for a man who abandoned you guys, and when I do—"

"Now you can't do what you are thinking, 'cuz if you do, then you'll be right back in here."

Langston's laugh surprised even him.

"So, what's new with you?"

"Well, just got a new job . . . at The Roz!"

"What? The Roz is open again! Well, I'll be." Langston trailed off in search of a distant memory. "Me and Mom used to hang there back in the day. That joint used to hop, I'll tell ya."

As Liza explained her serendipitous meeting with Eli, Langston took note of the twinkle in her eyes and started to make a comment, but she had already steered the conversation to her one obsession—his case.

"Remember how I told you about Professor Garrett?"

"Yes, of course." Sometimes Langston felt like he too was attending law school as she'd recount lectures about due process, proper cross-examination, and the prison-industrial complex.

"Well, he's starting an innocence project."

Langston let go of her hands.

"Billie, my appeals are up, we have to . . . *you* have to move on."

"Daddy . . ."

His heart melted when she called him that.

"Listen to me. There's always hope. We will," she paused to emphasize the next three words, "clear your name."

"That's all I've wanted, all I've prayed for from the beginning," Langston said, holding Liza's hands again. "But you've given up so much . . . too much. You need to focus on your daughter. It's not too late for you to start singing again. Nothing would make me happier. My prison should not be yours too. You have to move on." His voice cracked. "I'll be OK." He was lying.

Langston hated every moment of his existence.

Enduring the pompous guards and stale food was hard enough, but what grated on him most was the monotony. Each day he woke to twenty-three hours in the same cinder-block cell. It would be unbearable for any man, but Langston's innocence made the torment even worse.

The slow turn of every minute twisted his mind like the rubber band on a balsa wood glider as he replayed every moment of his trial through to the unbelievable and false conclusion, "We find the defendant . . . guilty."

As the judge thanked the jury, Langston had looked behind him. Elizabeth was in tears, but Liza sat with fire in her eyes. He knew then that she wasn't going to be able to move on.

Langston wanted freedom for Liza even more than he did for himself.

"Daddy," Liza derailed his runaway thoughts. "The innocence project wants to take your case. My professor, he's willing to make it a class project. That means you'll have a lawyer combing through your case, a team, actually, if you count the class full of wannabe lawyers. The best part? I can work on clearing your name as I complete my program. My degree could," she caught herself and adjusted that last word, "*will* save your life."

"Billie . . ."

"I know what you're thinking," she bulldozed her way past any objections, "if the professionals couldn't get you out, then what hope do we have? Daddy," she waited until he recognized her with his eyes, "I know your case better than anyone; it's my life."

Langston cringed.

"On top of that, I'm your daughter; no one believes in you more than me."

Langston sank into his chair and looked out the small window above Liza's head. A sparrow sat in its nest in the corner of the sill. Langston longed to trade places with that bird.

"I know how to get you out of here. I've got a plan." Again, she waited. "Remember how they got that cop acquitted? Remember how their clever display discredited those witnesses as the whole nation watched on Court TV?"

The bird flew away.

"Daddy, what worked for him could," she caught herself again, "*will* work for you."

Langston looked down from the empty nest.

He had come to grips with the inevitable. Langston was convinced that his—and Liza's—freedom would arrive only when the needle pierced his arm.

MASS FREEDOM

Eli continued reminiscing about Father Myriel as he worked his way through the never-ending tasks of opening The Roz. After school they'd hang out, sitting for hours in the old priest's study. Eli did his homework and learned to love learning as he watched the old priest read through stacks of books as he wrote his homily. When Eli noticed that his mentor's pen was down, he'd pepper him with questions, energized by the myriad of books that overflowed the shelves.

They had a game.

Eli would grab a book and randomly quiz Father Myriel about its color-coded, underlined passages.

"Who said 'By any means necessary'?"

"That's too easy, man, Brother Malcolm of course."

Eli was amazed that no matter what book he picked, Father Myriel knew the highlighted passages cover to cover and would often begin by telling Eli what side of the page it was on.

"Who's he?"

"Who was he? Well, I remember how he burst on the scene and gave all of us children of Africa a new understanding as to what it meant to be African *and* American."

"You knew him?" Eli asked.

"Nope, wish I did, but I followed him as best I could when it came to understanding what was up with America. Even his harsh words about us church folk ended up making us better Christians."

"What kind of last name is X?" Eli asked, looking at the cover of the book.

"Brother Malcolm was born with a different last name but he—like many others—felt that it didn't quite tell the truth about who he was, so he changed it to something more accurate. That was his problem, he always told the truth. That's why they shot him, fellow children of Africa, believe it or not."

"Why'd they kill him?"

Father Myriel fingered his crucifix. "We have a way of turning on the very ones that God sends to set us free."

After Eli marked another item off the list, he reached down the top of his T-shirt and retrieved that same crucifix.

He remembered how they were interrupted that day by Sister Francis letting them know that dinner was ready. As Eli packed up his schoolwork, Father Myriel said, "Hey, I thought that you could do the Gospel reading this Sunday."

Eli remembered how excited he was about joining his mentor on the platform.

That was the day Eli met Detective Slager.

* * *

Young Eli's voice trembled as it echoed over the old pews. He read the passage assigned to him by Father Myriel.

The Spirit of the Lord is upon me,
because he has anointed me

to proclaim good news to the poor.

He has sent me to proclaim freedom for the prisoners
and recovery of sight for the blind,
to set the oppressed free,
to proclaim the year of the Lord's favor.

"Thanks be to God," the congregation responded in unison.

"Good job, baby," Eli heard a woman say. He looked in her direction, but he couldn't find her face in the crowd.

Eli sat down as Father Myriel stood up. This was their favorite part.

"Brothers and sisters, the passage we just heard, read by our son," Father Myriel looked at Eli as he sat on his left. Eli's shoulders and cheeks warmed with self-conscious embarrassment knowing that everyone was looking at him. Turning back to his audience, the priest continued, "This passage is a declaration of freedom."

Eli cooled, for now every eye was on Father Myriel. The congregation had learned from experience that he wasted no words.

"A kind of freedom that can come only by a move of the Spirit."

"Amen . . ."

"A liberation for those who find themselves beat up and stepped on. It's good news for the shutout and turned away."

He looked at a woman sitting alone to his left, in front of Eli. "It's for your son . . ." turning to his right, ". . . your daughter." A thousand words were spoken in those glances.

"It's for you—for all of us.

"But even more than that, it is in you for those around you. The Prophet tells us that there is a kind of freedom that unlocks the locked-up, sustains the destitute, and provides light to those who live in the opaque corners of our world."

"All right . . ."

"Jesus hand-selected this passage as the text for his first sermon, and get this: After he explained it, do you know what happened?"

"Tell us, now . . ."

"The congregation present that day became so furious that they tried to kill the Anointed One!" He paused, meeting the eyes of several congregants before continuing. "They tried to throw him off a cliff . . . and do you want to know why?"

He glanced left at Eli and winked.

"Because we have a way of turning on the very ones that God sends to set us free." Eli smiled and recognized the line from their conversation about Malcolm X.

"Church, I tell you this so you'll be ready. Be prepared, because they will do to you what they did to him."

Silence.

"When we live for the freedom of others, we must be prepared, for the very ones we are trying to help can turn on us."

Eli put the crucifix back beneath his shirt and shook his head. Little had he known that just one week later he would use those very words to eulogize Father Myriel at his funeral.

* * *

At the end of the service, Eli stood on the platform next to Father Myriel as he dismissed the congregation with a final blessing. People headed downstairs for the after-service fellowship meal until just one other man remained.

"Officer Slager," Myriel said putting both hands on his shoulders, "so good to see you."

"Father, do you have some time?" asked Slager

"Confession or conversation? If it's conversation, then we can join the others downstairs and break some bread together. If confession," Eli noticed that both of them looked at the wooden booths in the back corner of the sanctuary.

"Confession," said Slager.

"Eli," Father Myriel called out as he walked to the back of the church with Officer Slager, "find Sister Francis. See if she needs any help."

Inside the confessional, Slager began, "Forgive me, Father, for I have sinned."

Neither of them knew that outside the booth, behind an adjacent cabinet, Eli stayed and listened.

THE EYEWITNESS

"We have to nail that eyewitness!"

"Billie, the deck was stacked against us from the beginning—"

"Daddy, listen to me—"

"No, listen to me. Remember how the city was spinning when the jury acquitted that cop. Do you remember what happened next?" Langston didn't wait for her to reply.

"'MOTHER'S DAY MURDERER STILL ROAMS FREE' was the headline. Mayor 'Uncle Tom' Stash sensed the uproar and the impending effect on his reelection, so what did he do? Called the press and threw down that audacious ultimatum: 'Justice will be swift. If I don't put the real perpetrator behind bars, then you should put me out of office.'

"Remember that? I do, because that's when the mayor, as an insurance policy on a second term, appointed that detective to make good on his promise."

"Daddy, I—"

"I didn't have a chance against him. Everyone knew that as a beat cop he was known for, 'bringing in his man.'" Langston made air quotes, the handcuffs limiting the distance between them.

"He was constantly harassing us in the Points, and they let him because he was one of us. And the media rewarded him every time. I know, I was delivering papers back then, and I can tell you, subscriptions went up when his chiseled black chin was featured above the fold."

Langston paused, and Liza jumped in.

"You're right. Something was up. I'm as convinced of that as you are, but I've figured it out."

Langston decided to sit back and listen, recognizing that she had driven more than 130 miles to see him.

"You're right about how Slager, at trial, said that he first started his review of the case by focusing on the alibis of formerly cleared suspects. He said that his theory was that the acquitted police officer was guilty but didn't act alone. It didn't make sense to him that one man could have out-smarted and overpowered all those guards. There must have been an accomplice."

Langston nodded.

"And he said that there was an eyewitness who reported seeing a black man wearing a baseball cap and sunglasses, running across the grounds of the state capitol building across the street from the bank at the same time the murders hap-pened. Detective Slager said that she, that witness, was the missing link.

"But get this, she's the weakest link in the case against you. It had been over a year since her brief encounter with that random black man on the capitol grounds. Over a year had passed before Slager had that woman interviewed by a sketch artist."

"Yeah, I remember, it was within twenty-four hours that that detective was back in front of the press saying, 'This is our man.' All we heard in Five Points was, 'This is our *black* man.' The next day they kicked in the door of our house, and do you remember what he did then? Slager and that Mayor Stash made sure the press was waiting as they led me through the front door of the police station, handcuffs and all."

"I know, Daddy, I know. But here's my theory. That eye-witness didn't identify you until after your arrest. All they had to go on was that she said she saw a black man running that day, and you were the only black security guard that was unaccounted for," Liza said.

"She must have been watching you on TV along with everyone else, and then when Slager called her down to the station and hustled her into the viewing room where they paraded you in front of her in the lineup, she picked you. Not because she recognized you from the day of the murders but because she had just seen you on TV. I'm convinced that Slager helped her too. Probably told her that they had plenty of evidence and that they just needed her to shore things up. Bet they promised her that you were caught red-handed."

Langston remembered that less than an hour after the lineup, he watched from his cell as Slager pranced before the crowd of cameras.

"We have our man. Langston Brown worked at the bank. Langston Brown had opportunity and motive. And an eye-witness just identified Langston Brown as the man she saw running from the scene of the crime."

"Daddy, you didn't have a chance, and here's why. Eye-witness testimony is not reliable."

He admired her fight.

"One time there was this woman who was raped, and then she identified the man who did it. He was convicted solely on her testimony. But get this . . ."

He admired her grit.

"Years later, another man's conscience got to him, and he came forward, confessed to the crime. He knew details that only the rapist could have known."

She paused to refocus.

"That woman is now an activist of sorts. Professor Garrett invited her to share her story with us in class.

"That's how they got that cop off. Remember in his trial, how the officer's lawyer showed that the bank employees were not reliable witnesses? Remember how they all said that the killer wore a hat, glasses, and a fake mustache? And remember how everyone in the bank vault identified the former police officer as the one who robbed them?"

She almost made him feel like he had a chance.

"But what did his lawyers do? Under cross-examination, they showed those eyewitnesses pictures of men disguised in the same way and asked the witnesses to identify them. None of them were able to say who the mystery men were. Even though one of the pictures was of the president of the United States and the other was acting superstar Indiana Jones himself, Harrison Ford.

"That's how the cop got acquitted. If they couldn't identify famous people in disguise, then how could they be so confident that they had the right man? That was enough for the jury to unanimously vote not guilty in favor of the former police officer. His lawyers did what your lawyers did not!" Liza pointed her finger so hard into the table that the tap of her nail echoed.

"We can do the same thing!"

Langston admired her hope.

CONFESSION

Eli heard everything Slager confessed to Father Myriel.

Eli had a bad habit of hiding behind the vestment cabinet that sat next to the confessional. If he were more mischievous as a teen, he could have wreaked havoc with the information he overheard. He knew which people were cheating on their taxes and whose marriages were on the rocks. Sometimes he almost fell asleep due to the lack of juicy details, but there was no risk of that today. Eli was all ears.

"Father, I'm trying to do right for our community," Eli heard Slager say. "You know why I went to the academy. You were there at my graduation."

Eli had seen the picture of Father Myriel pinning a badge on a younger Slager displayed prominently in his mentor's study.

"You were the one who got me into this."

"Yeah," said Father Myriel, "we knew we had to do something. Drugs had invaded, and crime was at an all-time high. The gangs ruled the streets, especially at night. So me and the other ministers organized a sit-in at the police chief's office. We demanded action. Shortly after that, they made Five Points into its own police district, and, as we demanded, they gave us officers who were from here and dedicated to the safety of this community."

"That's right, Father, that's why I joined. I wanted to make a difference."

"You are, my son. You may not feel—"

"You don't know what it's like out there. Those thugs have no respect. They're armed better than we are, and they're pumping poison into the veins of everyone they can, even our kids. They are not us." Eli could see that Slager spoke that last sentence through clenched teeth.

Eli sat in darkness next to the large wooden confessional box. The back of the box was made of plywood slats, with finger-width spaces between them. From his angle, he could see portions of Father Myriel's hands and feet. He could also see Slager's knees and the toes of his shoes. As he looked more closely, he could make out that the officer was looking down at a brown leather journal.

"How can I help you?"

Slager began to read, "I've . . . Father, I have sinned . . . I've framed a man."

Eli strained to see the reaction on Father Myriel's face but couldn't.

Looking up from his journal, Slager continued, "You know Dontel."

Myriel nodded a silent affirmation.

"Well, I've watched him terrorize this neighborhood for too long. The old folks won't go out at night because of him and his crew. They're scared.

"I know he's murdered people, everybody knows. But we've not been able to catch him. He's got an army of people protecting his black—" Slager stopped and looked up as if he remembered where he was sitting and with whom he was speaking.

"But I got him. Pulled him over the other night for speeding, could smell the weed walkin' up to the car so I got him out, couldn't believe he was alone. Father, this was my—no, *our* chance. So I cuffed him and put him in my back seat. As I searched his car looking for the drugs, I remembered the gun in my trunk.

"Earlier that night there was a drive-by shooting; two people died. All of us knew that it was Dontel's crew getting revenge for another incident that happened last week. Witnesses saw the shooter throw the gun out the window into a field a few blocks away. After searching for a bit, I found it. I still had it . . . hadn't tagged and logged it as evidence."

"My son . . ." Father Myriel whispered.

"If I put that gun in Dontel's car, he'd be off the streets for good." Slager was reading again from the leather journal. "Father, once that thought crossed my mind, I couldn't shake it. I knew what I had to do. If I could find the courage, I could and would save lives."

Slager looked up. "I know it was wrong, but what was I supposed to do?"

"My son, you have to make this right."

"I can't."

"You will not have peace until you make this right."

"We won't have peace until these thugs are gone." Slager again spoke through his teeth.

"You came to me for a reason. God forgives, and so do I, but you need to let me help you. I'll go with you."

Eli could see Slager through the slats.

"I'll think about it," he said as he threw the curtain open and left.

* * *

Eli looked across the street at the lunch line forming at Zona's. His mouth began to water as he recalled the hot links from the day before. Eli wasn't sure if he should share his Slager story with Liza; knowing that Slager was crooked but with no way to prove it might not be helpful.

Eli removed his work gloves and decided that he was hungry or, at least, hungry enough for another order of hot links.

As he continued to replay Slager's confession in his mind, Eli's heart rate spiked and his breathing went shallow. Terror flooded his body, and his instinct was to run back to his place and dive beneath the hatch door. His legs, however, felt like sandbags. The room Ferris-wheeled around him, and with each dizzying rotation Eli felt like he was falling fast with no ground in sight. He vomited on the sparkling floor; bile bittered his mouth. He forced himself to get within arm's length of the bar and braced himself with both hands.

Breathe!

His throat constricted.

Count!

His peripheral vision narrowed.

In, two, three, four . . . out, two, three, four . . .

Eli sat down on the closest barstool, trembling.

He wiped his face with the bottom of his sweat-soaked shirt.

Keep breathing.

He knew how to regain control. This wasn't the first panic attack prompted by his remembering what happened after Slager left the confessional that day.

BROWN'S BLUES

The large door opened, and Liza jumped.

Langston was used to the unannounced intrusions. He took one last glance at the empty nest outside the window and squeezed his daughter's hands.

Two guards entered the room. One was tall and clearly spent his off-hours working on his gym muscles; the other was bulky and had legs that appeared shorter than his torso.

"Time's up!" said the bulky one.

Langston stood, and they used the chain they brought with them to connect the handcuffs to his leg shackles.

Liza grimaced.

"Soon this will all be over. You'll be back with Mom, and we'll take Journey to the park, and you can push her in the swing and . . ."

The guards ignored her and ushered him out of the room.

"I love you."

"Love you too, Billie."

In the hallway, the guards started in.

"You know, Browny, the two of you's time is running out. Ain't going to be no walks in the park with your grandkid and that pretty little daughter of yours."

"Yeah, she is kinda pretty. What they call her type?"

In unison, the two guards started to sing, "She's a brick . . . house . . . She's mighty, mighty."

One of them began shoulder dancing.

Langston walked to the designated area for his pat-down and strip search. The tall guard felt Langston's chest, back, and armpits.

"You know the drill. Drop your drawers."

Langston pulled down his prison scrub pants and underwear.

He bent over, squatted, and coughed.

"You know who I'd like to be searchin' right now?" The tall guard started to sing again, "36-24-36!"

"She's a winning hand!"

"Enough!" Langston commanded.

The guards were startled into silence.

Stratling wasn't his only prison. He'd spent his first five years in Canyon City Corrections. There the guards were indifferent. When they escorted him to and from his cell, they were like robots walking a dog. Not so at Stratling. These guards seemed to think that it was their job to add to the punishment. Langston had had enough.

"Come on, you cowards, just you and me right here. You can even leave the cuffs on. I promise you, I'll still turn you inside out."

"Sounds like a threat, Browny. One more word and we'll put you in the hole."

"That's all you got? Threats? You know, on the outs, you would be pissin' your pants right now. I may be old enough to be your daddy, but you know you'd be shriveled and sha-kin', you know you wouldn't stand a chance. You don't stand a chance now, you know you shriveled right now, why don't you two drop *your* pants right now—"

"We're not playin'! One more word and we'll forget about you for a month."

They were telling the truth, and Langston knew it. The last time they put him in solitary, he was there for three months. The hole wasn't much worse than his death row cell: about the same size, the same food, just no TV and no visits. If they put him in the hole, then he didn't know the next time he'd see Elizabeth or Liza. Last time he missed Journey's birthday.

He hated the feeling of helplessness. Powerlessness.

Langston backed down.

The guards were silent as they made their way through the familiar maze. The only sounds were the automatic doors and the discordant slap of his dangling leg chains caused by his short, choppy steps.

"The human soul was not made to be locked up like this," he'd once told his wife.

His dehumanization was bad enough, but what incensed him was the thought of the guards watching his visits with his daughter like perverted Peeping Toms as they lusted after Liza.

Langston started to confront the guards again, but a childhood memory gently rescued him. After dinner, his father would head out to find a bottle to help him forget that he couldn't find a job. To distract him from his father's absence, his mother would help him memorize the poetry of Langston Hughes and reward him with small, foil-wrapped chocolates. He wasn't sure if he was named after the poet or if they just shared the same name. Either way, those evenings were among his most cherished memories from childhood.

They walked a little farther, passing the hall that led to solitary confinement.

Langston continued to think of his mother. Her love made him feel like he mattered. She had a way of making him feel invincible.

He stopped.

"'I've known rivers ancient as the world and older than the flow of human blood in the veins.'" Langston's voice bellowed, deep and steady.

The guards looked at each other.

"Brown, don't you start again," the short-legged one growled.

The tall one jabbed Langston in the kidney, and he started his shuffle again.

"'My soul has grown deep like the rivers.'" Langston's voice rose like the evening tide and filled the cavernous hallway.

"Brown, settle down," said the tall guard. The other preemptively radioed for help.

"'I bathed in the Euphrates when dawns were young. / I built my hut near the Congo, and it lulled me to sleep.'"

Langston was no longer present.

"'I looked upon the Nile and raised the pyramids above it. / I heard the singing of the Mississippi when Abe Lincoln . . .'"

He hunched.

The guard shouted, "Get that cell open!"

Langston stood tall; his shoulder blades touched as he flexed his back.

They dispensed with procedure, striking him in the gut. As he doubled over, they threw him on the ground, and with knees on his neck, back, and calves, they removed the chains.

Langston tasted blood in his mouth.

"'I've known rivers: / Ancient dusky rivers.'"

Four guards ramrodded him into his cell and slammed it shut. His toes caught underneath the door.

"'My soul has grown deep like the rivers.'"

Langston lay facedown. The memory of his mother forced its way through his rage and comforted him. He stood. Then paced. To the silver toilet and sink. Turned. To the bed. To the toilet and sink.

Again, he bellowed. "My soul has grown!"

He knew he had to help Liza move on.

"My soul . . ."

They must be prepared for the inevitable.

"My soul . . ."

Langston sank to the ground and curled up in the memory of his mother's lap.

MYRIEL'S MURDER

PTSD.

That was the diagnosis Eli received in his early twenties after battling paralyzing panic attacks, unpredictable nausea, and depression. The psychologist said that it was all due to a deep trauma.

When he was single, no one noticed, but when he and Antoinette married, she discovered the unforeseen wounds borne by her new husband. At first, she thought his lack of motivation and frequent disappearances were signs of a freeloader and secret womanizer. One day Antoinette followed him.

Eli went to a local park, and Antoinette fully expected to discover a tryst with another woman as she trailed behind him. Instead, she saw him drop to the ground in a fetal position, and—by the time she ran to him—he had hyperventilated himself into unconsciousness. With his secret exposed, Eli's symptoms began to display themselves regularly at home. His only reprieve came when he was in the ring fighting. It was Antoinette who finally convinced him to see someone who could help.

"You have a disorder of a magnitude that I've seen only in our soldiers returning from the battlefield. What happened to cause such entrenched and severe symptoms?" The shrink seemed puzzled.

The doctor concluded that the source of the trauma was Eli's lack of parents and life on the streets before Father Myriel took him in, but Eli—though he rarely spoke of it— knew the real reason.

* * *

After Slager finished his confession and left, both Eli and Father Myriel sat in stunned silence. All that separated them was a two-inch wall of wood and the evenly spaced slats on the back as they individually processed what Slager had said.

A police officer, one of their own, had just confessed to planting evidence.

In his shock, young Eli almost forgot that he was hiding. His racing heart threatened to disturb the silence, but it was the echo of his breath that alerted Father Myriel that someone was eavesdropping on the sacred moment of confession. Eli scooted deeper into his hole, hoping to avoid detection. The old priest gathered himself, drew back the curtain, and began to exit the box of confession.

However, a voice, from within the confessional kept him in his seat. "Father, forgive me for I am about to sin."

When did he? Wait, did he say, "about to sin"?

Father Myriel sat down, closed the curtain, and turned toward the man.

"My brother, I'm glad you stayed! Are you hungry? We have dinner downstairs," said Father Myriel.

Eli strained to see through the slats, but all he could make out for sure was the man's dark skin. He was no longer sitting at an angle that allowed him to see the man's face.

Is that Slager?

"I need more than a sandwich."

"Well, I'm here for the body and the soul," said Father Myriel.

"If I wanted that crap I would have come to the service!"

Eli didn't move for fear of making noise.

"My son."

"Stop calling me that. I came here for help, and all you offer me is a meal."

Eli then saw the shadow of the man lurch forward through the thin, silk opening.

"No."

The man said nothing.

"My son . . . please stop . . ."

Eli couldn't move.

Father Myriel gurgled.

Is he choking him?

Father Myriel was no match for the man's strength.

"I can't . . ."

The man's sweaty hands must have slipped off the old man's neck. Father Myriel ripped the curtain off the rod as he fell to the floor, his cane echoing as it rattled into silence.

Eli could see a little through the gap between the cabinet and the confessional. Father Myriel was on his back while the man stood above him, out of Eli's sight.

The man started to stomp.

At first, Father Myriel's hands softened the blows, but then the heel of the man's boot landed solidly on the old man's nose.

Stomp. Stomp. Stomp.

Father Myriel's head bounced off the floor.

He stopped moving.

Somehow, Father Myriel's hat ended up next to Eli.

Through the gap, Eli saw Father Myriel's chin and upper chest.

He's not breathing.

Silence.

Eli still had yet to breathe.

Run!

The man was still out of Eli's sightline.

Is he gone?

Terror and shock kept him from doing anything as Father Myriel's body recaptured his attention. Neither of them was breathing.

Then, footsteps. Moving in Eli's direction.

Fight. You have to fight!

"Father. Are you coming?" Sister Francis was making her way up the basement stairs.

Eli ran toward Sister Francis. He almost fell as his feet slipped on the blood of the only father he'd ever known.

The man was gone. While Eli never saw him, he was convinced he knew who the man was.

A week later, Slager arrested another gang leader for the murder of Father Myriel and was promoted to detective. Young Eli, however, knew the secret to his success. Slager was a good cop gone bad, a man who had crossed the line from loving his community to preying on the very people he was sworn to serve and protect.

Young Eli was convinced that the man Slager presented as the murderer was only a cover for his own sins. Eli was even more convinced that Slager knew that someone had been hiding behind the confessional and that it was only a matter of time before he returned to silence him.

* * *

This is why Eli was grateful to make his bed beneath the floor of the storage building. It made him feel that he had a place to run when he thought his past might come looking for him.

As Eli recovered from the panic attack, he contemplated what to do when Liza arrived for work.

He wondered when or if he should tell her what he knew about the detective who put her father on death row.

His heart raced as panic leaped back on him. He hoped she didn't find him in this condition.

DELAYED GRATIFICATION

Eli straightened the bottles behind the bar as the city inspector made his rounds.

Today Eli hoped to receive the final stamp of approval so he could make opening night in three days, as advertised.

"Hey, boss, those bottles haven't moved since you put them there," Liza said from across the room.

Eli pointed toward the back and then placed the same finger across his lips. "Shh. He's going to hear you."

"Hear what? I wasn't talking about him, I was talking about you."

Eli felt self-conscious that after a week she had already been around long enough to notice his idiosyncrasies.

"I'm just nervous, and when I am, I straighten things."

"Sounds a little OCD to me," Liza shot back.

More than a little!

When Antoinette convinced him to seek help with his panic attacks, the doctor diagnosed Eli with moderate levels of obsessive-compulsive disorder in addition to his post-traumatic stress disorder. In the months following her death, Eli almost obsessed himself to death.

She thinks this is bad—compared to a year ago, this is nothing.

"Boss, come here. Which do you like better?"

Liza had two different place settings displayed for him.

"This one is more modern and chic, while this one pays homage to the heritage of this place. What do you think? Should we go with the past or the future?"

Eli never knew how to answer questions like this. As she pressed him for an answer, all he wanted to do was straighten the salad fork that wasn't quite parallel with the other utensils and perpendicular to the edge of the table.

"Liza, you don't know how grateful I am that you walked in here a week ago. I had no idea what I was going to do about these sorts of things."

Eli adjusted the fork.

"These decisions are yours. Pick the one you like."

"OK, boss, but don't say I didn't ask."

Eli enjoyed her spunk.

"Mr. Stone," the city inspector emerged from the back room.

Eli was never the handyman type. When it came to the remodel of The Roz, he didn't know what he didn't know. To cut costs, he attempted to do the work himself and hired help only when trial and error had failed him. Eli now wondered if cutting corners would cost him.

"Well, Mr. Stone, what do you want first, the good news or the bad?"

The inspector didn't wait for a response. "Well, the bad news is that you didn't pass inspection."

He handed Eli the clipboard with a long list of items. The word *failed* appeared too many times for him to count.

"Please sign here acknowledging that you understand that you cannot open until these items are addressed."

Eli scribbled his signature, and the inspector gave him his copy.

"Thank you, Mr. Stone, and here's my card. Call me when you're ready to schedule a follow-up appointment. Any questions?"

"Yes," Eli replied. "What's the good news?"

"Oh yeah, the good news is that me and the boys back at the office are rooting for you. Sure hope you can pull this off."

Eli read through the list as the inspector showed himself out.

Three days. There's just too much. We'll never make opening day.

Liza snatched the list from Eli's hands and made her way toward the door. The steady sound of her boots announced her departure.

She turned back toward Eli. "Boss, it's going to be OK. We got this."

Her jeans were the last thing Eli saw as Liza left.

THE DECISION

The next morning, Eli beat the sun to the sidewalk. The city inspector's words were still in his head—"Me and the boys back at the office are rooting for you. Sure hope you can pull this off."

As he approached The Roz, he noticed a man standing on the sidewalk, peering through the window.

"Brotha, this your place?"

"Sure is. How can I help you?"

"I hear you need some work done—"

"Yeah, but I can't—"

"Liza sent me. Can't stay long, though, gotta get to the work site by 8:30. I only have a couple of hours."

The man grabbed his toolboxes as Eli opened the door.

"My brotha, point me to the furnace."

Eli showed him the relic, red tag and all.

Throughout the morning, Eli welcomed a steady flow of men with toolboxes—plumbers, a couple of electricians, and even a welder. Each used Liza's name to gain entry.

After a mid-morning lull, a second wave arrived around noon, and—a short time later—Liza made her entry with pizza boxes in hand.

"Who's hungry?"

A chorus answered back, "Billie!"

Eli watched as she placed their lunch on the bar and made her way around to each man, greeting him with a hug of gratitude.

The aroma of mozzarella and pepperoni drew everyone into a circle with Liza and Eli at the center.

"Everyone, thank you soooo much for coming here on such short notice. Thank you. Thank you. *Thank you*."

Nods of love and affirmation rippled in her direction.

"You know we're here for you. And you too, Eli—we got you," said one man.

"Well, bon appétit everyone, and don't forget, the check's in the mail."

"Billie!" Another chorus.

The men crowded toward the lunch, leaving Eli and Liza to themselves.

"Told you. We got this." She winked.

"You weren't lyin'. But who's Billie?"

"Oh, just a nickname from my singing days."

"The check's in the mail?" Eli shifted from the small talk.

"Don't worry, boss."

"Liza, I am worried. All morning there's been workers here fixing all of my mistakes. I don't have any margin in the budget. I'm spread thin, way thin. If I pay them, then I can't pay you or—"

"Relax. We—you, me, them—we all got this."

She continued before Eli could.

"These men," she gestured with both hands while turning in a circle, recognizing the workers who were heading to their spots with pizza in hand, "these are all friends of Daddy's. All I did was go down to the shop where he used to cut hair and put the word out. That's why they are here."

She paused.

"They're here because of Langston Brown."

Eli took it all in with Liza.

"So, no worries. You won't have to pay them much at all."

"Much?"

"Well, I did make them all a little promise."

"Liza, how much?"

"A reserved table on the night of their choice, an appetizer, and . . ."

"And?"

Liza turned toward the bar and the wall of bottles.

"And three drinks each."

Eli nodded at the bargain as they stood shoulder to shoulder.

For the rest of the afternoon, Eli worked alongside whoever needed an extra hand and marveled at all the tricks of the trade he observed. Tricks he could have used over the past year. He also took his fair share of good-natured ribbing as his mistakes and shortcuts were laid bare before these professionals of the trades.

When the sun set and the sidewalk darkened, the remaining workers headed home to their families. Some were off to second jobs.

Eli finalized the schedules for the kitchen crew and waitstaff and posted them in the back room. Liza even made the inspector reappear for the final sign-off and certificate of occupancy.

Opening day was upon him, and Eli was ready.

The Roz sparkled like it was 1949.

The bar glistened, and each tabletop was a work of art thanks to Liza's much needed feminine touch.

The old place felt new.

After Liza finished cleaning up a mess left by one of the workers, she organized the hostess station and polished the signature banister that led to the balcony seating. Then she turned her attention to Eli.

As Liza walked around the back of the bar, Eli wasn't quite sure what to do next. Should he offer a hug? A handshake? If she were Antoinette, he'd have kissed her. He decided not to shift the direction of his feet and kept himself facing out over the bar.

Liza sidled up beside him and joined him in admiration.

"Thank you," Eli said.

"Congratulations," said Liza.

On the stage, across the room from the bar, stood a tall young man with short dreadlocks. He was setting up for the band.

"Hey, Tyrone, you ready for this?"

The man looked toward Eli with his Ethiopian eyes and, without hesitation, chirped, "Pops, I was born ready!"

Eli liked his new saxophonist and bandleader. The young man had a respect for the old standards and a love for the new horizons of hip-hop. Eli hired him with the hope that he'd be a bridge between the generations.

Just then the door was flung open, and a young couple entered with their three children.

Eli shouted as he ran from behind the bar and hugged the light-skinned, golden-haired woman and high-fived the rest.

"Whatcha all up to?"

"Opening day," said the woman's husband. "Thought we'd stop by to see if you needed any help."

"'Bout time," Tyrone said from the stage.

"Listen here, big brother, come down off of that stage and see if I don't whoop you with your own saxophone," said the littlest of the clan.

Tyrone jumped down and swooped her up as he pretended to eat her chin.

Eli put his arm around the woman—Antoinette's sister.

"So can we help?"

"Of course," said Eli. "Many hands make light work."

Eli turned to Liza, "Everybody, this is Liza. Liza, this is family . . . Do we need help?"

"Hi, family," Liza motioned. "Absolutely. Still need to hang some things, and the back room could use some organizing, boxes everywhere."

"All right then, sounds like we definitely could use some help."

Liza went to grab some supplies, and the siblings began to jab at one another as they followed Tyrone to the stage.

"So how you doing?"

"I'm good." Eli feigned conviction.

"Yeah?"

Eli didn't respond.

"And, tell me about her," said the golden-haired, light-skinned woman.

"Her," Eli looked pointedly, "is my new employee."

"That's all?"

"That's all."

"Well, she seems nice, and this seems like as good a time as any to remind you that Antoinette wanted you to move on."

Eli glared.

"I know. I know. Don't shoot the messenger. You know she made me promise to tell you that at least twice a year, and—brother-in-law—my duty is now complete for this year."

Liza returned and started directing traffic, and everybody got to work.

Then, without warning, Liza grabbed her coat and purse and ran out the door.

Eli started to follow her, but the TV above the bar grabbed his attention.

Governor Stash was holding a press conference; Detective Slager stood behind him.

The crawl at the bottom of the screen read "BREAKING NEWS: LANGSTON BROWN TO BE EXECUTED—30 DAYS . . ."

PART II

Why should it be *my* loneliness,
Why should it be *my* song,
Why should it be *my* dream
deferred
overlong?
—Langston Hughes

HEART-TO-HEART

Two days had passed since Langston's friends made light work of the city inspector's list and the governor announced the day of his execution.

When Liza left The Roz that night, she called everyone she could to get more information. Her professor convened an emergency meeting with the lawyers of the newly formed innocence project. They, along with Liza, strategized for hours and formulated a plan of attack.

After the meeting, Liza tried to comfort her mother.

"Mama, don't give up. We have a plan. There's still time."

"Politics! These things always come down to politics. It's an election year; guess he needs to get some votes. *Our* mayor is *their* governor now."

"Mama—"

"Billie, they are going to kill your father. My heart is broken too. I don't know how I'm going to survive without him, but you have to face what is happening. This is how they do us. We need to be there for him. He's gotta face this horror, but we will make sure he doesn't face it alone."

She understood that her mother was just trying to prepare her for what she saw as the inevitable, but Liza wasn't ready to face those facts of life.

Liza hadn't spoken to Eli since her abrupt departure, but she—along with all the staff at The Roz—knew that he lived half a block south, behind the restaurant, in the old renovated storage room. She headed there.

Liza knocked on Eli's door just as it was opening.

A tall man, not Eli, with curly brown hair and well-traveled eyes towered in front of her, a metal box tucked under one of his two sleeve-tattooed arms.

"Is Eli home?"

"Mr. Stone," the man yelled back into the home, "there's a lady out here."

The man stepped past her as Eli emerged.

"Thanks, G," Eli said. "And nice work, you're a true artist. When can you finish it?"

"Don't know. We'll see," the man said as he turned the corner, ducking his right shoulder as the rest of his body followed.

"I shouldn't have." Liza now regretted coming to Eli's home. She felt as if she was intruding, like she was crossing a line.

"It's OK. That's G, the best tattoo guy around. The only problem is that I never know when he's going to be around. A little unreliable, but his work is worth the hassle."

"So you're gettin' some more ink. Can I see it yet?"

"Na, not yet. It's still a work in progress."

"It's addictive, isn't it? Once you start, you can't stop." With both hands, she pointed at the tattoo of the thirteen-hour clock on her chest. "This one's far from my only one."

Liza's inked right arm was proof of that.

"You ain't lying. Something about the planning and dreaming about decorating your body. But as odd as it sounds, my favorite part is the p—"

"Pain!" Liza joined in. "Yes, I try and explain it to others, but they just don't get it."

They both stood on the front stoop for a moment. It had been a while since Liza had met someone who understood this aspect of her life. She was an artist, and her tattoos were a way of expressing herself. Singing was her first love, but with the imprisonment of her father and her pursuit of his vindication, she had little time for her dreams. For her, a tattoo was a sacred expression of her soul. The pain was difficult to endure at times, but she loved the beauty that it produced. Her body art gave her hope that the other pains in her life would someday result in something beautiful.

Before Liza could figure out how to keep talking about their pain, Eli saved them.

"I was worried about you."

"I'm sorry for leaving like that."

"No worries. Would it help to talk about it?"

Liza nodded, and Eli, looking a little unsure as to whether or not to invite her in, gently suggested it with a side-nod of his own.

Liza hadn't known what to expect about Eli's home but certainly not this. Her eyes surveyed the sparse room. Questions abounded as she took in the small studio-like room with its wood floors and white walls.

She tried not to appear obvious as she took inventory of the few items she could see: the brown-skinned figures in the painting on the wall, the kitchen with toaster oven and coffee maker, Eli's hat on her right, next to the radio.

Her eyes eventually settled on the table with its candle and lighter.

No couch? Where does he sleep? Where's the bathroom? Bedroom? Windows?

"No need to apologize," he said.

Liza's eyes struggled to focus on him.

"I saw the news. How are you doing?"

"We're in shock." Liza was thinking about her mother and daughter.

"Even though we knew this day might come, we weren't ready—" Liza interrupted herself, "And thirty days! How did they come up with that? They're going to kill Daddy in thirty days?"

Liza knew what she needed.

"We're close. The innocence project has taken the case, is going to file a motion. And that witness, we're going to get her on the stand and . . ."

But Eli was her boss.

"We are not giving up. There's still time . . ."

Liza didn't remember Eli drawing near to her, but as she sank into his arms, his warmth comforted her. They said nothing.

Her eyes drifted to the table set for two.

Mr. Stone, who are you?

"I'll be there," she whispered. "Tomorrow night."

It had been a long time since she had let herself be held, a while since a man instinctively knew what she needed.

How did he know?

"It's opening night. I promise. I won't let you down."

Liza lifted her arms and allowed herself to hug him back.

Thank you.

As her head rested on his chest, she wondered if Eli could feel the racing of her heart because she could hear his heart pounding out a strong, steady, frantic song.

OPENING NIGHT

"The children of Africa will come home tonight. Or, at least, home as we know it."

Eli stood on the stage with his staff assembled before him for a last-minute pep talk.

Outside, the crowd waited four abreast along the sidewalk, all decked out in their Sunday best.

"I can't thank you enough for joining me on this journey," Eli continued. "Tonight, we become a part of history. Diz and Duke stayed and played here. Out front right now, the old folks are telling stories about when our musicians came through town. How they made their money in downtown Denver playing for the children of Europe, but they made their beds here in Five Points. In return for the hospitality, they would perform for almost nothing, here, at The Roz. Nothing but the dignity of being able to walk through the front door."

"I hope you know we ain't playing for almost nothing!" Tyrone snorted. His band laughed and nodded.

"May your tip jar overflow," Eli said with a smile.

"I mean that for all of you. I hope we can make a good living together, but I also hope that you feel the higher purpose behind what we're doing here."

Eli took the time to look each person in the eye as he surveyed the faces of the cooks, waitstaff, and band.

He settled on Liza. Yesterday—after the hug—Eli surprised Liza with a promotion. Manager. She had his trust.

"I want to say a special thank you to someone who has been a godsend to me. Without her support and hard work these last couple of weeks, we would not be where we are."

All applauded. They knew the person he was referring to and the recognition she deserved. Liza smiled and nodded at Eli before she diverted her eyes to the floor.

"Soon this place will fill with smiling, seemingly well-put-together people. Do you know why they're here?"

"To have a gooood time!" Tyrone almost slapped his own back.

"Yes, they're here for a good time, but they could find that at any number of places around this city. So why are they coming here, to Five Points?

"They've come to The Roz because here they are free from that which makes them feel like they have to live up to a never-defined standard. They've come here tired and worn out by life out there. Once again, Five Points has a place for each of us to catch our collective breath. That's why they and we are here."

Eli and Liza again made eye contact.

Once his words settled, she dismissed the staff to their respective assignments.

With Liza running point on logistics, Eli was free to hold court from behind the bar.

After one last look-over, it was time to open the doors.

Eli made his way toward the crowd bustling outside.

"Hey, Tyrone."

"Yes, Mr. Stone."

"You gonna give me some Dexter tonight?"

"Nope, gonna give you some of me tonight!"

"All right then, let's do this! Show me what you got."

The band began to play, and as Eli opened the doors, the people waiting outside erupted.

Eli wished Antoinette were standing at his side.

*   *   *

There were a few hiccups, nothing major, especially for an opening night.

Eli watched as Liza ironed out a communication mix-up between the front of the house and the kitchen and then made her way around the room, giving special attention to the workers who'd arrived in force to collect their three drinks.

Behind the bar, he felt alive. Almost happy.

Having Liza allowed him to tend to more than people's drink requests. At the moment, Eli focused on an elderly woman who sat alone, bobbing her head.

"How are we doing down here?" Eli asked.

"I'm fine, thank you."

Eli poured her another drink.

"This one's for Frank. He would've loved to be here with you."

Eli turned to find that Liza had slipped behind the bar and was watching him.

"You are doing for her what you did for me when I walked in here."

Eli put the bottle back in its spot.

"Is that really why you opened this place?"

Eli wasn't ready to answer a question like that.

"Tell me, Mr. Stone, what did you do before The Roz? Who were you before all of this?"

"Ms. Brown, this is my bar. Do you know what that means? I'm the one who gets to ask the questions," Eli replied with a wink.

* * *

The Roz started to empty as couples eventually remembered their beleaguered babysitters and summoned the strength to venture back outside Five Points. Eli made his rounds, affirming the staff, beginning with the cooks in the kitchen, then making his way to the tired waitstaff as they reset their tables for the next night. After patting Tyrone on the back, he turned his attention to Liza.

"Thank you."

She nodded and smiled without showing her teeth.

"I know tonight couldn't have been easy for you, but you were remarkable."

"It wasn't, but it would've been harder if I didn't have all of this to distract me. I just can't figure out why now."

She wasn't distracted anymore.

"The timing doesn't make sense. There has to be something else going on."

Eli thought so too. At the press conference, Governor Stash announced that every death row inmate would be executed with "as much haste as legally possible."

"Why now and why not start with any of the others who've been sitting there long before Daddy arrived? It doesn't make sense."

Eli shook his head in silent agreement.

"And the promotion," Liza launched in a different direction before Eli could react to her last statement, "you have no idea how much that means to me."

"Not only can I use the money, but—trust me—I know how important this place is to you. I won't let you down."

"I know you won't," Eli said as he walked behind the bar. He grabbed a bottle of wine and two glasses.

Liza sat down.

"I have a question for you."

"Sure, anything." Liza leaned forward.

"Would you mind locking up?"

Eli knew that Liza wanted to debrief and share stories about how the evening went, but if she was disappointed by his request she hid it well.

"Here's a key and the code to the alarm panel."

Before she could respond, Eli was out the door—wine and glasses in hand—headed for home.

Eli had a prior engagement.

Antoinette.

COCKTAIL OF DEATH

The next day, Eli left Five Points.

He woke up early, and before climbing the ladder, he went a couple of rounds with the heavy bag to prepare his heart for what he might encounter.

During his fighting days, he found that if he prepared his mind then his body would follow. That worked for opponents in the ring, but now, when he had to face the unseen forces of society, he'd discovered that preparing his body for a fight readied his mind. And for Eli, leaving Five Points and engaging with the children of Europe was a fight.

The morning was warm, and the streets were abuzz with life. Children scurried to catch the bus as parents chased them down the sidewalks with forgotten lunch bags and last-minute hugs.

Eli set out walking west on Welton Street, and after a few blocks, his internal monitor alerted him that he'd moved out of Five Points and into downtown Denver. He'd had friends who called him paranoid, a reverse racist. Antoinette even worried that he would join the Nation of Islam. Eli had considered it for a bit, but ultimately he didn't believe in all the UFO stuff and talk of a mother ship coming to rescue him.

Keep your guard up.

He forged ahead, south, down Broadway, past the City and County Building, courthouse, and art museum. After purchasing a breakfast burrito from a corner vendor, he continued.

Langston's fast-approaching execution date occupied his thoughts as he eyed his destination on the opposite side of the street—a one-story brick building with large red neon letters that read "The Weekly Word."

Eli entered through the tall glass door and approached the front desk.

"Good morning, Mr. Stone," the lady greeted him.

"'Mornin', Alice. How was your trip?"

"Had a blast. We'd always wanted to take a cruise, and now with the kids gone, it was like a second honeymoon."

Eli chuckled as he looked down the hall.

"She's in her office, Mr. Stone."

"Anybody with her?"

"All clear. Feel free to head on back. You know she always has time for you."

Alice winked.

He walked past the sales team readying themselves for their cold calls and the reporters scurrying to meet their deadlines.

The door to the corner office was open. Inside sat a tanned white woman wearing a white broad-collar blouse with her toned legs crossed and visible beneath the glass-topped desk. Her long blond hair rested behind her ears as she sat reading, red pen in hand.

Eli knocked next to the nameplate that read merely "Fredricka."

"Whatever you want, the answer is 'no,'" the woman said.

"Are you sure about that?"

Eli's voice triggered a Pavlovian reaction; her pink tongue licked her red lips.

"Check that," she said. "The answer is 'no' *unless* your name is Eli Stone. For he, on the other hand, can have whatever he wants."

She stood up and adjusted her black pencil skirt, and after moving her blond hair from behind her ears, she made her way around the desk, tapping her manicured fingers on the glass.

She hugged Eli, long and slow.

"Well, Mr. Stone. Have a seat." She motioned to the couch.

Eli sat next to the armrest as Fredricka took the center cushion.

Eli sat with both feet on the ground, hands clasped around the brim of his hat on his lap. He knew what he was walking into.

"Congratulations on opening night," Fredricka said, letting her hand squeeze his shoulder.

How does she always end up in the lead of a conversation?

"I wish I could have been there, but I hope you know that he was." She nodded in the direction of the cubicles.

Eli had noticed that the city's most influential restaurant critic was sitting high and aloof in the balcony the night before. He made sure that Liza triple-checked his orders before they left the kitchen and waited on him personally.

"Is that why you're here? Do you want a peek?" She paused for effect as her tongue ran across her lips again. "Hmm, do you want a peek . . . at the review he's writing about the grand reopening of the historic Roz supper club and bar?"

Eli shook his head no.

Fredricka leaned in. Eli felt the heat of her breath. The sweetness of her perfume triggered memories.

"Don't you at least want to know the headline?"

Eli shrugged his left shoulder where her hand still rested.

Curious as he was, he attempted to shift the direction of the conversation. "Actually, I'm much more interested in what Mrs. Messay is working on."

The Weekly Word was known for its hard-hitting, fact-soaked stories on the inner workings of Denver. Roberta Messay was the city's finest investigative journalist and the star of the team of writers Fredricka had assembled.

"So tell me, what story do you have assigned to her?" he asked.

"Eli, I was hoping this was a friendly visit." She pouted her red lips and then kept pressing. "Eli, I know what you need. You and I were a good thing, and though we didn't work out, that was then and this is now. We've grown." She was still pouting. "Mr. Stone, let me help you with your broken heart. I know what you need." Her hand moved to his thigh. "Why don't you come out of that cave of yours and warm up at my place?"

Eli put his hand on hers to stop the caressing.

"Freddy, I'm not here for that."

"I love it when you call me that. You know you're the only one who's allowed to—"

"Freddy, I need to ask you a question."

He could still feel her breath.

"Go ahead. Anything."

Eli removed her hand from his leg and turned toward her. His bent left leg now created space between them.

"What do you know about Langston Brown?"

She sat back and crossed her arms; her blond hair hung like parted curtains on either side of her face.

"Arrested. Convicted. Set to die soon, very soon."

"Yeah, tell me something I don't know."

Eli was now leaning toward her.

"Freddy, I know you're on this. You had to have sensed that something was odd about that press conference. Governor's up for reelection, and so he invites the cameras to his office and, flanked by Slager, announces that he's going to expedite the executions of everyone on death row. What do you make of that?"

"The desperate machinations of a man who feels his power slipping away," she responded.

"Maybe." Eli studied her. "But why now, and why start with Langston Brown?"

She looked down.

"Does this have anything to do with the fact that his daughter is working for you at The Roz?"

Eli's eyebrows arched. "So you are on the case. I had no doubts. You're the most connected gadfly in this town."

Fredricka placed her finger in the center of Eli's chest and pushed him back into the corner of the couch. She leaned forward. He could feel her toned thigh between his.

"You're going to owe me one for this."

She got up and closed the door to her office.

Turning back to Eli, she said, "Midazolam, pancuronium, and potassium chloride."

Eli arched his eyebrows again.

"The cocktail of death."

EXPIRATION DATES

Eli rode the bus back to Five Points.

It had been a few weeks since his last panic attack, but after what he'd learned from Fredricka he was desperate to get back to the safety of the melanin-saturated streets of Five Points before something happened.

With each passing block, his mind ran circles around what he'd just learned.

Eli had grown used to Fredricka's overtures. When Antoinette died, she was the first to arrive on his doorstep with a baked lasagna in hand and the last to leave the reception after the memorial service.

Antoinette's sister warned him, "Be on guard. A wounded man like you is a hot commodity in the eyes of the divorced and lonely. I promise you, brother-in-law, there will be no shortage of women who will try to move in on you. They're already jockeying for the opportunity to occupy the vacant space in your heart."

Fredricka quickly discovered that as far as Eli was concerned, there was no space left open after Antoinette's passing. That, as far as Fredricka was concerned, was only a temporary situation, and she was determined to be the first person Eli turned to when he emerged from his cocoon of grief.

"Whenever we ask questions, we must be prepared for the answers to disrupt our lives," Eli whispered under his breath, quoting from a book in his underground library. The bus stopped, allowing two teens playing hooky to jump on, skateboards in hand.

Eli was not ready for another disruption in his life.

After Antoinette's death, he retreated from everything and everyone. For months he locked himself in the house they'd built together in East Aurora and wouldn't answer the door for anyone. When his mailbox overflowed with consolation cards, the mail carrier stopped delivering and taped a notice on his door as to where he could find his correspondence. He lost weight to the point of emaciation. His friends and family worried, but there was no way in.

Eli wanted to die.

At the funeral, the pastor remarked, "The magnitude to which we love someone is matched only by the magnitude with which we hurt when they are gone." Eli loved Antoinette lavishly and without limits, and when she died he paid the price for that love.

Eli still wants to die.

When Eli emerged, it was to purchase The Roz and its adjacent storage room. He sold their house, took all the life insurance proceeds, and combined that with a loan to obtain the dilapidated property that developers had passed on for years.

Eli knew that renovating The Roz and returning it to its former glory was a long shot, but he desperately needed something that would occupy his every waking moment.

That was three years ago, and everyone who knew Eli knew that he had yet to address the depth of his pain. Eli knew it too.

Eli circled the headline of the article that Fredricka gave him: "THE DEATH COCKTAIL."

"Eli, this is top secret, and it's just a rough draft. We're still fact-checking it and looking for the smoking gun. You can't show this to anyone." After Eli agreed, she reminded him, "You're going to owe me for this, but I promise we'll both enjoy it."

Eli wished he didn't have to rely on Fredricka, but she was the only one who might know why Langston was set to die in less than a month.

He'd been right; there was something behind the sudden announcement. Fredricka had summarized it for him, but now he began to read.

For years the electric chair was the preferred method of execution in the US. However, after a few botched high-profile events where the inmates literally burst into flames, the public lost its appetite for the burning flesh of the guilty. The electric chair was deemed cruel and unusual punishment, a violation of the Eighth Amendment. Politicians sought to strike a balance between those who believe that the death penalty is necessary and those who seek to outlaw its use on constitutional grounds.

Lethal injection was the compromise.

For this means of execution, an inmate is strapped to a gurney, and after speaking his or her last words, a deadly potion of three drugs—midazolam, pancuronium, and potassium chloride—is administered. The first renders the convicted unconscious. The second paralyzes. And the third causes cardiac arrest.

As the bus passed the justice center, Eli felt ill.

"Expiration Dates."

He circled the two words so many times that the ink bled through to the page underneath.

The three drugs used in the death cocktail are not easy to come by; most municipalities have to purchase them from other countries.

"It appears that Colorado's supply of death drugs is about to expire, and they want to use them before they go bad," Fredricka told Eli, back on the couch in her office. "I've got Roberta working on the corroborating evidence so I can publish the story. But this is why they are expediting the executions. The death cocktail is starting to stink like curdled milk."

Expired drugs increase the odds of excruciating pain during the execution, violating the convicted's constitutional rights.

Eli got off the bus and joined the brown faces headed toward Five Points. All walked fast, as if they were holding their breath underwater after diving too deep and were now trying to make it to the surface before they blacked out.

When he arrived at his place, he burst through his front door, opened the hatch, and made his way down the ladder, skipping the bottom three rungs entirely.

Fredricka didn't know why they picked Langston to go first, but Eli had a hunch it was Slager's doing.

Eli turned on the shower, undressed, and jumped in before the water even had a chance to warm up.

No time with his books. No workout. It was only midday, but Eli needed a shower.

CLOSING TIME AGAIN

The Roz had only been open for a week, but routine had already set in. The band and staff split their tips and were out the door. Only Liza and Eli remained, addressing final closing tasks.

"All done," Liza said, coming out of the back room.

"Just about wrapped up here as well," Eli said from behind the bar.

He grabbed a bottle of wine and a couple of glasses.

"All right, boss, see ya tomorrow. I'll lock up," said Liza.

Eli, however, had decided to postpone his date with Antoinette. After his time with Fredricka, he wanted to talk about Langston's case. He placed the glasses on the bar and poured.

"So, catch me up," he said.

"Project Joseph is up and running and has made Dad's case priority number one," she began without hesitation.

"Project what?"

"Project Joseph. That's the name of our new innocence project. They had a naming contest, and my submission won. How cool is that?"

"Congrats—who's Joseph?"

"From the Bible, he's the guy who got accused of a rape he didn't do and was put in jail. In the end, he found his freedom and was still able to live a full life."

Eli knew the story well. He'd heard Father Myriel preach on it many times, and the words of those sermons immediately came to mind: "What happened to Joseph is what's happened to the children of Africa in America. He was sold into slavery by his brothers and imprisoned due to no fault of his own, but—" the congregation always joined in at this point—"but what others meant for bad, God meant for good: the saving of many lives."

Eli missed his mentor. More of his teaching came to mind: "So don't grow bitter. Just realize that ultimately we are here to make things better," Father Myriel would conclude.

Eli always struggled with that last part.

His attention returned to the present as Liza continued, "Our lawyers are queued up and they're even allowing me to sit in on strategy meetings." She sat down and took a drink of the red he'd poured her. "We only have three weeks to save Daddy's life . . ."

"So what's the plan?" Eli was now thinking about the cocktail of death.

"We're going to put that eyewitness on trial," almost spilling her wine as she gestured. "There's no way that woman saw Daddy that day, and we are going to prove it."

Eli hoped that Fredricka would release the story in time. There would be a public outcry if people knew that the real reason they were expediting the executions was that the drugs were expiring like rancid meat.

Five Points would explode.

"Do you know that every man on Colorado's death row is a child of Africa? It's not that the children of Europe don't commit heinous crimes, but they usually ended up with a life sentence or were found not guilty by reason of insanity." Eli had read an earlier exposé by Roberta Messay.

"Tell me about it! And look at you, soundin' all like a professor!"

Eli also suspected that Slager's role was more than political opportunism. The expiration dates, in and of themselves, didn't seem like enough of a reason to fast-track the executions. Eli was convinced that Slager was covering his sins.

"So tell me about this eyewitness. Why is she the key to your dad's freedom?"

"To begin with, eyewitnesses are beyond unreliable. My professor dedicated a whole class session to debunking them. For instance, when they're trying to pick a suspect from a lineup, police often give cues with their body language or make suggestive remarks that influence the witness as to which person to pick. They can even lead the eyewitness to the person they want them to choose by how they stack the pictures. In one case, all the pictures were black and white except for the one the detective wanted to highlight; that one was in color. Not all cops do this on purpose . . ." Liza paused to finish her glass.

"Who's soundin' like the professor now?" Eli interjected.

Liza raised her empty glass.

As Eli refilled it, he thought about Slager. He was sure that if there was witness tampering, it was on purpose.

Liza picked up where she'd left off. "When you add time to the mix, all bets are off—the more time that passes, the less able any of us are able to remember what we saw. That's one reason why I think we can get her. That eyewitness identified Daddy months after the murders. There's no way you can trust that. Especially when you add race to the mix. That lady was white. They've done experiments, and guess what? To the average white person, we all really do look alike!"

"This all reminds me of Rubin 'Hurricane' Carter.'" Eli made his voice sound like a fight announcer's.

"Whoa, who's the Hurricane?"

"He was one of my heroes back when I was a boxer—"

"You were a boxer? Do you still get in the ring? Is that what keeps you lookin' all svelte?"

"No. I mean, yes . . ." That last comment had Eli on the ropes. He started over. "No, I don't box anymore, but *yes*, I'm still fighting—every day. And thank you.

"Anyway, Hurricane was a fighter back in the '60s who served twenty years for murder. I read his biography where he tells about how at first no one picked him out of a lineup but then an eyewitness later identified him as the shooter. After a few trials, they discredited the eyewitnesses. I hear Denzel is even making a movie about it."

"Well, when we're all finished, they'll make a movie about Daddy too!"

Eli hoped she was right, but deep down he wasn't sure if it would be a thriller or a horror flick.

"So what's next?"

"We're filing an emergency motion tomorrow, and if all goes well, the judge will agree to hear our plea."

Eli wanted to tell her what he had learned about the expiration dates, but he knew that Liza would only take it to her lawyers. Fredricka had asked him to keep things quiet as they confirmed the facts behind their suspicions.

Eli raised his glass. "May the truth prevail."

Liza nodded.

"Who knows where help may come from?" Eli said, turning out the lights.

Outside, Liza stood next to him as he locked the door. The streets were silent, and the stars were bright.

The deadbolt clicked into place, and Eli turned. They stood silently for a moment.

"I'll wait till you get to your car," he said.

As she drove away, Eli continued to watch.

LAWYER'S MOTION

The next day, Eli sat in the courtroom next to Liza and her mother. She had invited him, Eli thought, for moral support.

They sat directly behind Langston, with a polished wood barrier between them. Langston kept turning to see his wife and daughter. Beads of sweat congregated atop his bald head. Occasionally one ran down the back of his head, like a sinner down the aisle to the altar, where it was absorbed by the collar of his blue dress shirt.

"You look dapper," Liza whispered.

Langston smiled. A seeming rarity.

His smile turned grim when a tall black man entered the courtroom. He wore a suit, tailored to accentuate the width of his shoulders in comparison to his waist. As he walked down the center aisle, he unbuttoned and removed his coat and strutted on a catwalk of his own making.

It was Slager.

Out of instinct, the hairs stood tall on Eli's arms. The last time he was in the same room with Slager, he had been a young teen, hiding, witness to a murder. Eli now regretted being in the courtroom. *This is the man you've been hiding from your whole life. What if he recognizes you?* He took a few deep breaths to avert a panic attack and avoid causing a scene. His eyes returned to Slager, and though the detective briefly glanced at Eli he didn't seem to recognize who he was.

Maybe he doesn't remember me?

"All rise!" The bailiff called the room to order.

The door to the judge's chambers swung open, and once all eyes settled upon the vacant hallway, the judge made his entrance. He moved with the gait of a giraffe as he climbed the three steps to his black high-back chair.

Another bead of sweat made its way to Langston's neck-line. Liza leaned toward Eli.

After an unnecessarily long pause, the judge finally spoke. "Thank you. You may be seated."

The judge acknowledged Langston's lawyer. "Counselor. I've read your motion. You may address the court."

"Your Honor, we are here because an innocent man has yet to receive justice."

"Objection." Apparently, the DA was going to challenge everything.

The DA stood. "Judge, the defendant has received all due process. He was found guilty by a jury of his peers and has exhausted all his appeals. And," he tried to swallow without pausing, "might I remind the court that the true victims, the families who lost loved ones during this horrendous act, have yet to receive the satisfaction that justice promises them."

Mr. Goodstein, Langston's lawyer from Project Joseph, tried to interrupt but the DA pressed on over him. "Furthermore, the citizens of this state have spoken. Some perpetrators are so depraved that they must be held accountable before God and society by surrendering the very breath in their lungs." The DA sat, satisfied that he had delivered his speech as practiced.

"Mr. Goodstein," the judge turned to Langston's lawyer. "Your esteemed colleague is correct in that your client was tried and found guilty by a jury of his peers and has exhausted all his legal options."

"Your Honor, given the makeup of the jury, I would beg to differ that Mr. Brown sat before a jury of his peers."

Eli—along with everyone in Five Points—noted that when the former police officer faced trial, his jury was composed entirely of the children of Europe. But when Langston's jury was seated, not one child of Africa was present.

"But I digress," Langston's lawyer continued. "Your Honor is aware of the unprecedented announcement made by our governor. Most likely for political reasons, it has been determined that every person on death row will be executed without further delay." He paused and looked squarely at the judge. "I submit that we can all agree that this is a court of law, not a court that is swayed by the whims of our elected officials and their desire for a second term."

"Your Honor, here *you* are the higher authority, which is why we are here and not at the governor's mansion."

Liza squeezed Eli's arm.

Eli was impressed with Mr. Goodstein; he'd done his homework on this judge. Flattery was the way to his heart.

"On what grounds do you make your request?"

"Your Honor, these are unprecedented times, and we call on you, and you alone, to make an unprecedented decision."

The judge wasn't blinking.

"We ask that you grant a stay of execution. Langston Brown deserves the same benefit of the doubt that the former defendant, the police officer, received. He was able to meet his accusers in court, and my client deserves the same."

Still not blinking.

"In Mr. Brown's case, the key eyewitness was withheld, hidden and tainted. She has never testified under oath under penalty of perjury nor has she had to withstand the scrutiny of cross-examination."

"Judge," the DA standing again, "there has been ample opportunity for—"

"Withheld!" Langston's lawyer boomed. "Her name, whereabouts, and existence remain withheld to this very day."

The courtroom was as silent as the middle of the night.

Both lawyers started to speak.

The judge waved them off with a flick of his hand. The sleeves of his robe trailed across the papers on his desk.

"Is she available to testify?" the judge asked the prosecution.

"Ahhh . . . yes . . . yes, Your Honor."

The judge looked down. Eli wondered if he was weighing his own political aspirations.

"One witness. One week from today. Motion granted."

The gavel clacked and the judge stood.

"All rise!"

Langston turned toward his wife.

Liza prayed.

Eli stared at Slager.

Slager wrote something in a leather journal that looked like the one he'd held when he confessed his sins to Father Myriel.

THE SHOW MUST GO ON

Slager left the courthouse immediately after the hearing and headed straight for the governor's mansion, a stately, plantation-like home in the heart of Denver. He knew that he needed to reach the governor's ear before the evening news.

"I can't believe that judge!" Governor Stash shouted at him after he'd provided a quick recap of the events.

Spit flew onto his desk, landing just shy of Slager.

"I didn't appoint him so he could someday go rogue."

Slager tried not to look at the saliva drop in front of him.

"How can we be tough on crime if we don't have judges with the intestinal fortitude to follow through?"

Slager now noticed the rest of the spittle clinging to the untrimmed whiskers of the governor's trademark mustache. Stash was a man with a widening figure who wore suits tailored to his former self. His belly hung over his belt, hiding the buckle. His colorful suspenders were more functional than fashionable. In college, he'd decided that his last name, Stash, needed to become a reality on his upper lip. From afar, the governor's mustache looked like the black paint the football players apply under their eyes. Up close, it looked just as fake. Despite the ridicule he endured in the Sunday morning editorials, he kept it and made sure that a mustache was featured prominently on his campaign yard signs that plastered the city.

"Sir, there's no way Brown is getting out of this," Slager interjected, peeling his eyes away from the governor altogether.

They'd known each other for years. Slager was Stash's secret weapon during his years as mayor. Stash promised everyone that he would protect them and put the bad guys in prison. Slager made sure the promise was kept. They had a don't ask, don't tell policy. The governor didn't ask how Slager was always able to bring them in, and Slager wouldn't tell if he did. "Plausible deniability," he once told Stash, though the governor knew that his future ambitions relied on Slager's secrets.

"How can you be so sure that Brown will get the needle? The people of this state need to see not only that we can catch and convict them but that we can see the job all the way through to the day we strap 'em to the gurney and send 'em to hell."

"He's guilty of the Mother's Day Massacre," said Slager. "The public's on our side. There's no way that judge is going to reverse things. They'd drag him and any political aspirations he has through the proverbial streets if he did."

"What do you know about this witness?" asked the governor. "Are there any surprises I need to prepare for?"

"She's solid," said Slager. "Back then, she was a typical middle-aged housewife. Today, the kids are grown and she's still married to the same man. She's normal. Believable."

"Then why did we," the governor looked around as if to check for eavesdroppers in his own office and lowered his voice as if he'd spotted one, "why did we not tell the defense about her?"

"She wasn't material to the case," Slager answered quickly, in an attempt to boost his credibility. "When the jury heard that Langston Brown worked every Sunday morning except the one when those people got murdered, it was a slam dunk. Plus the jury didn't believe his alibi. Langston said he was at home the whole time preparing brunch, but his own wife testified that she slept in past the time that the murders were committed. The jury clearly saw that he had a window of opportunity."

"But what about the witness?" Stash pressed.

"She picked him out of a lineup, but in the end, we didn't need her to make our case."

"Does that mean we shouldn't have disclosed her?"

"That was the DA's decision," Slager responded, passing the buck.

Langston Brown wasn't Slager's only secret on death row. The more executions that happened, the more dead the skeletons in his closet became.

"We'll get Brown. We need to press on with the plan."

The governor thought for a second, then asked, "Who's next in line?"

Slager immediately suggested Jerome Jefferson, the man he'd arrested for the murder of Father Myriel.

"No, we should save him for last," the governor said, shaking his head. "What about Duncan?"

Ann Clifford was a beautiful young mom who, after a girls'-night-out dinner with her sister, was ambushed as she walked to her car, which was parked behind the restaurant. The man muscled her into his paneled van, then beat and brutalized her. After weeks in the hospital, she went home pregnant with the perpetrator's child. It was widely thought that Nathan Duncan was guilty of that crime, but Ann Ratcliff wouldn't testify against him because she wanted to protect her newborn son from knowing that he was the product of a rape. Duncan went free but eventually found his way to death row for the rape and murder of another woman.

They both nodded in silence, then the governor picked up the phone and dialed Stratling Correctional Facility.

"Warden, Duncan's next. And no need to delay—four days. The execution will happen this Friday."

Slager left, his journal tucked under his arm.

BEYOND BAD

The families sat in adjacent rooms staring at the curtain-covered glass that separated them from the death chamber.

They could hear the prison personnel rustling in the room beyond the glass. As they listened to the muffled sounds, their imaginations filled in the blanks.

In the chamber, the warden directed his guards like an air traffic controller.

They had rehearsed this moment multiple times the day before and three times that morning. But now it was for real.

Nathan Duncan walked into the sterile room, legs and wrists restrained, flanked by two guards. A third guard walked behind with the priest in tow. Duncan's knees gave way at the sight of the cruciform-shaped gurney that lay in front of him.

As the guards removed the chains, Duncan looked around. Even if he could muster the strength to run, there was nowhere to go.

"I'm going to need to you to slide up on the gurney," the guard said flatly. Those in the witness rooms strained their ears.

"Head there," the guard pointed. "Feet here."

Duncan complied and, as he lay back, began to gasp for air, the sound of his strained breathing echoing in the room.

The guards tightened and buckled the restraints with choreographed precision. Duncan started to sit up, but it was too late; he was fastened tight with the black leather bindings. He'd lain down for the last time.

The priest drew near. "Relax, my son."

Duncan looked up.

"God forgives. Trust in him."

"I . . ." Duncan came to himself and cursed everyone, including God.

Even as Duncan's remorseless words flowed, the priest began to pray. "Our Father, who art in heaven . . ."

Duncan's vile words continued.

"Hallowed be thy name . . ."

Duncan looked at the priest, venom in his eyes.

The priest continued praying, in part in an attempt to distract Duncan from the needle pricking his arm. But Duncan felt the needle's insertion, and his head spun around, locating the culprit.

He aimed and spat. The nurse writhed back, wiping her face.

"Spit shield," the warden commanded. A guard appeared out of nowhere and pushed the mesh mask over Duncan's head. His head spun again, straining to bite the man.

"The vein collapsed, I can't find it," the nurse said, frustrated.

"Hold your composure," the warden said.

The warden was now the object of Duncan's glare.

"Proceed to plan B."

Duncan was nude under the hospital gown. The nurse lifted the gown to find another vein in his groin.

She endured his rude propositions and gyrations.

Finding the vein, she stabbed the needle into place.

Duncan heaved bile onto the spit shield. The families were still unable to see what was happening, the curtains still covering the glass.

"If I could, I'd tear you to shreds, and I'd like it." Duncan almost giggled. She believed him.

Behind the two-way glass stood two stoic volunteers with two sets of three syringes on the counter in front of them. One set contained a harmless saline solution. The other held the death cocktail. Neither knew which would be responsible for Duncan's death, though afterward, both would brag that each had been the one.

"Relax, my son, you're going to be OK."

Sweat pooled under Duncan's body; the leather pad was now slippery.

The warden picked up the phone. "Governor Stash, we are ready. What is your will?"

After a brief moment, he nodded and hung up the phone. "The governor has given his authorization. Continue with the execution."

One of the guards looked down at Duncan. "Mr. Duncan, I'm going to clip this microphone on you, so's everyone can hear your last words."

And then, without warning, the gurney began to tilt until he was in an almost upright position. The two sets of curtains then opened, revealing the two witness rooms.

"Mr. Duncan, you have been found guilty of rape and murder. We would like to give you the opportunity to make a statement before we proceed with your sentence."

Feeling caged and exposed, he focused on his mother.

"I'm sorry, Ma. You deserved better." She was the only one in his room.

Looking toward the other room, "Hope you find peace." Then the attack began, "Hope this makes you feel better! Huh? Will it? Huh?" Duncan was now beginning to shout.

The guards moved in and lowered the platform in an attempt to calm him.

"Go to hell." Duncan focused on the guards. "You . . . and you . . . and all the hell of ya!"

"Proceed now," the warden ordered. "Proceed."

Both volunteers picked up the syringe marked #1 and squeezed the plunger.

The midazolam made its way into Duncan's vein. The sedative began to take effect.

Duncan stopped fighting. Stopped yelling. Everyone started to relax.

"Administer number two."

The volunteers complied, but as the drug raced into the vein, Duncan's eyes popped open.

"Hots. Hots. It's hot!"

The warden, sensing trouble, muttered, "What's going on in there?"

Duncan screamed and attempted to lift his heavy head.

"Hots. It's burning. Like fire. It's hot fire."

His body seemed to slither as it convulsed. His teeth clacked. His eyes rolled back, lids fluttered.

"He's supposed to be sedated, paralyzed," the warden shouted. Then he ordered, "Close the curtains."

"Sir, do you want us to cease?"

No response.

"Sir, his eyes are open. Do you want us to stop?"

"No. Number three. Administer number three."

Later, the warden would tell the press that "the needle inadvertently slipped out during the inmate's excessive agitation and writhing."

When he read this quote in the paper, Eli figured that the death cocktail must have already expired and gone bad.

It took thirty minutes for Duncan's heart to stop.

During the whole ordeal, behind the two-way glass, Slager stood in the corner.

DAY IN COURT

Liza sat holding hands with her mother with Eli on her left as before. She tried to connect with him, but he was preoccupied with someone else in the courtroom, staring at a detective who sat behind the lawyers for the prosecution.

Liza had never seen Eli so agitated.

Langston's lawyer stood and addressed the bench.

"This is it, watch," Liza interrupted Eli's surveillance.

She could have asked the questions herself. For the past week, Liza and the lawyers refined the interrogation. In an attempt to prepare for every scenario, they even did a couple of mock run-throughs with Liza playing the part of the eyewitness. She had every question and possible answer and possible counters to those answers memorized, and she was confident that this was the moment that she'd worked for all these years.

"Your Honor, may I approach the witness?" Langston's lawyer inquired with great deference.

News of the botched execution was on everyone's mind that day. Especially Langston's. He told Liza that some of the guards taunted him with the gory details.

"Hots! It's hot!" They had cackled as they mimicked Duncan. "Boy, when we put that needle in your arm, it's gonna burn like fire."

Liza fumed when she found out but knew the best course of action was to win this battle, so she prayed.

Langston's lawyer stood next to the eyewitness and handed her a piece of paper. "Do you recognize this?"

"Yes, it's the sketch of the man I described," she replied.

"Is that an accurate portrayal of the man you saw that day?"

"Yes." She was nervous, and her voice communicated that as well.

"Any idea why you weren't called to testify at the trial?"

"Objection. Calls for speculation." The DA stood.

"Sustained." The judge looked at Langston's lawyer. "Stay focused, Mr. Goodstein."

"So this is the man you saw that morning?"

"Yes, it is."

"How can you be so sure."

"Objection. Argumentative."

"Mr. Goodstein." The judge glared.

"Ma'am," pointing to the sketch of the black man wearing sunglasses and a baseball cap in the sketch, "do you see this man in the courtroom today."

"Yes," she said and pointed at Langston. The DA sat back in his chair.

Eli finally looked at Liza. "It's OK. We've got this," she whispered.

"Let's talk about when you identified Mr. Brown in the police lineup that day."

Liza leaned forward.

Lady, you don't know what's comin'.

114

"Did you have any reservations about whether or not he was the man you saw running on the grounds of the Colorado State Capitol the morning of the murders?"

"No. I know it was him."

Are you sure?

"Then can you explain why you failed to identify Mr. Brown the first time police showed you his picture?

"You will recall that the day after the robbery, police showed you and all the other witnesses pictures of every guard who had worked in the bank over the past year. Mr. Brown's photo was among the dozen or so Polaroids you reviewed."

She hesitated. Goodstein continued.

"Do you remember when the police and FBI brought a stack of pictures to your home?"

"Yes."

"That was the day after you saw the man running near the intersection of Broadway and Colfax, correct?"

Correct.

"Correct."

"Why didn't you identify Mr. Brown then, when your memory was crisp?"

The witness folded her arms. "The man that day didn't have a mustache, but in the picture he did."

It was true that Langston had facial hair in varying degrees while he worked at the bank and that he shaved the night before Mother's Day because his wife liked him without his whiskers.

Who cares if he had a mustache or not?

"Do you mean to tell this court that the mustache on Mr. Brown caused you not to recognize him?"

"That's right," she affirmed. "It made him look different."

"Then how are you certain that you are correct now? Didn't the man you saw that day have sunglasses and a hat? Why didn't that obscure your ability?"

"Objection." The DA just wanted to interrupt Goodstein's flow.

"Overruled," the judge quickly countered.

All right, just stay the course.

"Ma'am," Goodstein was now back at the podium. "Isn't there another reason why you identified my client in the police lineup?"

She shook her head.

"Please answer out loud," the judge reminded her.

"No. I know what I saw."

Goodstein pushed on. "What time did you arrive at the police station for the lineup?"

"I . . . I don't know exactly. Mid-afternoon."

Liza looked at Eli. Eli was watching someone else.

"Wasn't it around 2:30 PM?"

"That sounds about right."

You know that's right.

"What were you doing prior to that?"

"I'm not quite sure." The witness now had the look of a squirrel caught in the middle of the street with a car fast approaching.

Come on now, don't make this more difficult than it has to be.

"Well, let's slow down. How did you know that they needed you to come down to the police station?"

"I received a call from Detective Slager."

"And where were you when you received that call?"

"I was at home."

And?

"Did you have the TV on?"

"I probably did."

Gotcha!

"So you saw the breaking news like everyone else?" It was a question, but Goodstein made it sound like a statement. "You saw Mr. Brown led into police headquarters without a mustache or sunglasses or a hat, didn't you?"

Liza held her breath.

The witness fought for composure but didn't answer.

"Didn't you?"

"Objection." The DA rose to his feet. "Badgering the witness."

"Overruled."

"Your Honor, please instruct the witness to answer the question."

He did so.

"Ma'am, did you watch the breaking news on TV before you identified Mr. Brown?"

"I'm not sure. I might have."

Mr. Goodstein walked back to his seat and stood next to Langston.

"Your Honor, I think this would be a good time for us to take a break."

All agreed. Especially the DA.

The bailiff brought all in the room to their feet as the judge exited.

Slager bolted.

Liza hugged her mother and smiled at her father. "Told you," she mouthed.

Eli followed Slager.

DENIAL

During the break, Eli watched Slager pace in the smokers' courtyard. Slager was in the midst of an animated phone conversation. The more he waved his arms, the more confident Eli became that his suspicions were correct. The cross-examination had him riled up.

Slager looked in Eli's direction a couple of times but without reaction; it was as if he was looking through Eli. Slager seemed oblivious to the fact that Eli had been Father Myriel's young protégé.

After the allotted time, court reconvened, and they were all back in their seats.

Hope filled Langston's side of the room; apprehension hovered over the other.

The eyewitness waited on the stand.

"Counsel," the judge addressed Mr. Goodstein. "Are you ready to proceed?"

"Yes, Your Honor."

Liza still held hands with her mother, but Eli felt her shoulder pressed into his. Eli leaned back in her direction, even thought about putting his arm around her but didn't.

The Browns had been waiting for this moment for more than a decade. He felt privileged that Liza included him for what most likely would go down in Denver's history.

Eli remembered how in the first trial, the former police officer's attorneys exposed the eyewitnesses that fingered him as the murderer. They showed the eyewitnesses pictures of various celebrities disguised as the perpetrator inside the bank on that Mother's Day. Even though they showed the witnesses the president of the United States and a few movie stars, the witnesses couldn't identify the suspects with half their faces hidden by a photoshopped hat and sunglasses. If witnesses couldn't even recognize famous people in disguise, then how could they have been so confident that it was the former police officer who robbed them that day?

Liza told Eli that the plan was to employ the same tactic in Langston's defense. The eyewitness identified Langston even though the man she saw running was wearing a baseball cap and sunglasses. Liza and a volunteer paralegal from Project Joseph had spent the past few days preparing displays for their experiment.

Michael Jordan and Denzel Washington were household names. Everyone in America knew who they were. But would the eyewitness recognize them if they were disguised just like the man who ran past her that day?

Liza was convinced that she wouldn't. Eli hoped she was right.

Eli eyed her hard work as it sat on the table in front of Langston and his lawyer.

Photos of Jordan and Denzel were glued to pieces of cardboard, with photocopied sunglasses and baseball caps taped over the top half of their heads, so they looked like the man the eyewitness described for the police sketch of Langston.

Liza even tried the experiment on some of her classmates, and the majority of them failed to identify the famous faces underneath the disguise. Eli failed too.

"Your Honor, may I approach the witness again?"

The judge allowed.

"Ma'am," he said, handing her the same sketch of Langston as before. "Let's pick up where we left off."

The DA's arms were folded atop his belly.

"This is the sketch of the man you saw the day of the crime, correct?"

"Yes," she said, slightly annoyed at the repetition.

"And it is your testimony that Langston Brown looks like that man, correct?"

"Yes."

"Even though the man you saw running that day was wearing a baseball cap and sunglasses, you are convinced that the man you saw that day and Mr. Langston Brown are one and the same, correct?"

"Correct," she said.

Liza pressed even harder in Eli's direction as she continued to hold her mother's hand with her left hand while reaching across her body with her right arm and grabbing Eli's hand.

Mr. Goodstein walked toward his table. "Your Honor, I'd like to introduce exhibits 1A and 1B—"

As soon as the DA saw what the exhibits were, he shot to his feet. "Objection!"

The whole courtroom saw what was coming next. The eyewitness's credibility was about to crumble.

"Mr. Goodstein, what are your intentions?" the judge asked, already knowing the answer.

"We only seek to test whether or not the witness can truly identify someone wearing a hat and sunglasses."

"Objection sustained."

Eli wasn't sure he heard what he heard.

Did he just say "sustained"?

Liza sank.

"No. Oh, God. No," she whispered, but her breath was coming out with the force of a scream.

Wait, what? Overruled. Surely, he meant to say "overruled."

"Your Honor, with all due respect, there is precedent—"

"Sustained." The judge picked up his gavel.

"Your Honor, the last judge in a prior case allowed—"

The gavel slammed down, its blow echoing. "I am not that judge, and I will not allow my courtroom to become television drama!"

"But Your Honor—"

"Counsel, my decision stands."

Mr. Goodstein looked at Langston. There was nothing he could do.

Eli noticed that the eyes of the eyewitness were fixed on the exhibit.

While the judge and lawyer went back and forth, she could see one of the pictures. She looked as if she was struggling to identify the person beneath the disguise.

Langston's lawyer noticed too.

Langston's lawyer looked at the DA and slowly began to peel off the taped sunglasses to reveal the face beneath the disguise.

"Mr. Goodstein." The judge spoke as one speaks to a child about to throw a rock at a window.

Langston's lawyer continued to peel off the photocopied sunglasses until the eyewitness saw the face of the man who would go down in history as the greatest basketball player of all time. All eyes were on her. The look on her face told the truth; she would have failed the test.

"Mr. Goodstein," the judge now stood, growling with teeth clenched, "I will hold you in contempt if you do not stop this mockery at this very moment."

The gallery was becoming unsettled. "Order in the court!"

The judge slammed his gavel down again.

"Counsel, do you have any more questions for the witness?"

Mr. Goodstein, knowing that he had nothing else, replied, "No, Your Honor. Defense rests."

Turning to the DA, "Would you like to cross-examine the witness."

"Yes." The DA stood, then had a moment of clarity. "Actually, Your Honor, the prosecution also rests."

"Very well then," the judge said. "You can expect my decision tomorrow. This court stands adjourned."

Goodstein turned to console his client. Langston was looking at Elizabeth. Liza collapsed, arms still crossed, into the support provided by Eli and her mother.

Eli wondered if she was thinking what he was thinking.

Fire. They're going to fill Langston's veins with fire.

STRANGE FRUIT

In the foothills overlooking the Denver metroplex is a place of solace known as the Mother Cabrini Shrine, maintained and prayed over by the Missionary Sisters of the Sacred Heart.

Sister Francis took Eli there after Father Myriel's murder with the hope that the tranquil setting would, over time, soothe his trauma.

Deer grazed, and rabbits scurried. In the winter, the local buffalo herd came down from higher altitudes and wintered nearby. Eli loved to ride in the back of the groundskeeper's truck and drop bales of hay for the herd as it surrounded the vehicle. He couldn't believe how puppy-like the massive beasts were. Their personalities didn't match their stature.

It was here that Eli grew into manhood as the nuns beamed over him, especially Sister Francis.

She was a round, portly woman with wrinkled, porcelain skin.

"Big-boned," she would tell Eli.

"I come from hearty stock that traded the cold of northern Europe for the cold of New York City."

She had bright red hair streaked with gray. But what Eli loved, even to this day, were her gray-blue eyes. They had a way of making him feel like everything would work out in the end.

The Mother Cabrini compound was a series of small dormitory-like buildings arranged in a circle around the main building, which housed the chapel for morning and evening prayers, a kitchen, a dining hall, and a lodge area with a ceiling-high fireplace.

Each evening after dinner, the nuns would gather for tea as the fire roared. Eli and Sister Francis always sat closest to the flames.

Here they remembered Father Myriel.

"He loved you like a son," she would say. "The son he never had."

Eli knew she felt the same way.

Once she told Eli of a man she loved and how he asked her to marry him. At first, she agreed. "But then I remembered my higher calling. It broke my heart to break his. As much as I loved him, there was a greater love that beckoned me."

Her voice would then quiver. "God put me on this planet for a reason. To help people, and now, to raise you up and make sure that you're OK."

The glow of the fire illuminated Father Myriel's books. It took months to move the library up here. When sadness struck, Eli would read them, and because he was sad often, he devoured the whole collection.

"You know they're yours," she would remind him. "Padre loved your love for learning; he'd want you to have them."

Mother Cabrini's was good for both of them.

One night, a couple of years after Father Myriel's murder and about a year before Eli left the womb of the Missionary Sisters of the Sacred Heart, he finally summoned the courage to ask the question that had haunted him since the murder. They had processed the details of that day—the blood and the stomping—many times. But Eli had another question that went beyond the mere fact of the murder. When Eli asked, he wasn't sure if he wanted or was prepared to hear the answer, but he blurted it out nonetheless.

"Why did he, of all people, murder him?"

When Slager arrested someone else for the murder, young Eli's nerves were far from calm because deep down he believed Slager was guilty and the arrest was just a cover . . . and that it was only a matter of time before he was next. Convinced that Slager would return to silence him, Eli began to sleep underneath his bed with a steak knife from the cafeteria within reach. However, he never shared his theory with anyone for fear that Slager would find out.

Tonight, though, Eli wanted to know. Reading Father Myriel's books had him thinking about the way the world works, and he always knew that Sister Francis was up for those kinds of discussions too.

As the fire popped, Sister Francis began her response, "I know what you are trying to get at, but I think you're asking the wrong question. You are asking 'why' when you should be asking 'what.'"

"I don't understand . . . what do you mean?"

"You want to know *why* that man, of all people, would have murdered Father Myriel? Asking 'why' is like driving down a dead-end street hoping to get to where you want to go. It rarely delivers. The better question is '*What* caused that man to do what he did?' While the road is difficult, at least it leads somewhere."

Sister Francis was an immigrant to this land. "One of the children of Europe," she would say. That's how everyone who spent time around Father Myriel referred to race. Father Myriel had felt that it was a made-up construct and that if we were going to get past our preoccupation with race then we need to start at the beginning and recognize that we all—except for the native peoples—originated beyond the confines of America. "While we are all American, we are more than Americans," he would preach.

Sister Francis continued, "My people crossed the Atlantic in search of a better life. Mom and Dad risked everything and arrived with nothing but the hope of having something for which to hope. They struggled and survived and were happy that we children would grow up in this land of opportunity and freedom."

While Sister Francis was grateful for her parents' sacrifice, she no longer saw the country with the same optimism as her mother and father by the time she reached adulthood.

During the time of life when her peers were marrying and starting families, Francis was searching for a different path. "It was then that I saw the picture that changed the course of my life," she told Eli on many occasions.

"Two black men, Thomas Shipp and Abraham Smith, hanging from a tree in Marion, Indiana. A mob sledgehammered them out of jail and beat them. They were accused of murder, robbery, and rape, and the vengeance-thirsty throng placed nooses around their necks. When one of the men tried to free himself by pulling the rope from his neck, they broke his arms."

The picture sickened her—two young black men, hanging, crooked necks, both bloodied, one without pants. Later the woman would testify that they did not rape her. What Francis found unfathomable was the crowd. It appalled her that they performed this atrocity out in the open—even posed for pictures, without masks—with no fear of retribution.

"I heard a voice," she would say later. "It told me that I had to do something. That I couldn't just be a part of the crowd. No action in the face of injustice is injustice too."

Eli had heard her tell the story of the picture before, but that night by the fire she added a new detail. "It was then that I realized that there was something sinister at work between us—the children of Europe and the children of Africa. That's why I became a nun. That's how I ended up working with a black priest and living among Africa's offspring in Five Points."

"Sinister. What do you mean sinister?"

Eli watched as she grabbed the fireplace poker and rearranged the wood.

"Ahh, this gets to the heart of what happened to Father Myriel. There is this thing that we have infected you with. A sickness that we possess that we have passed on to you."

"Who?"

"The children of Europe."

Eli stared at the fire, trying to make sense of what she was saying. He knew that Sister Francis had a way of turning a simple question into a classroom lecture. He was determined to stick with this conversation because he'd learned that her lectures usually paid off in the end.

"The children of Europe. We brought it with us," Francis continued. "It was like a latent virus waiting for the perfect petri dish. America was and still is the ideal environment for it to thrive.

"Think about what happened at the foundation of this country, the willingness we had to kidnap millions of your people to create the Land of Liberty.

"How ironic," she said. "Can you imagine that first child of Africa who arrived here in chains? If he could have understood English and asked, 'Where am I?'" She shook her head. "He would have fainted from the irony when he heard the answer, 'You're in America, the land of the free!' But we justified it!"

Sister Francis was unusually comfortable speaking in the plural, including herself in the sins of her ancestors.

"We invented whole philosophies and theologies to make it so. We needed you to become black so that we could become white. That ensured our manifest destiny; that little intellectual invention solidified the advantage we needed."

Sister Francis paused to see if Eli was tracking.

Young Eli struggled to comprehend.

Then a question formed in his mind, "Racism? Are you are saying that racism is the reason that man murdered Father Myriel?"

"Not quite, my son, but you're on the right track."

Francis got up and started a pot of hot water for tea.

"Remember how you felt about the rabbits?" Sister Francis asked.

THE WHITE TEACHER

A log popped in the fire.

The wildlife that surrounded the convent was bountiful—geese landed on the lake during the winter, squirrels of the long- and short-hair variety hopped limb to limb, deer and bighorn sheep strolled, wild turkeys were heard but not seen. Most of all, rabbits, for the presence of people kept fox and bobcat away and allowed them to flourish.

After Eli moved to Mother Cabrini's, he isolated himself in the barn for hours at a time. There he discovered a litter of rabbits and began to help their mom keep up with their endless appetite by sharing his stowed dinner vegetables.

They'd grown used to young Eli's presence, and due to the lack of predators, there was no flight instinct in them at all. As he sat next to them and their hollows in the hay, he felt safe.

"What do you mean?" Eli was unsure as to where Sister Francis wanted to take the next portion of the conversation.

"What did you feel about the rabbits?"

"I don't know. I liked being around them."

"Why?" she asked, Socratically.

"They made me feel good. I enjoyed everything about them—their soft fur, long ears, and endless energy."

"Would you say that you loved them?"

Eli nodded.

"And how did you feel when you heard a fox was spotted a ridge away by some of the sisters when they were out on a hike?"

"I was worried for them and wanted to protect them."

Sister Francis started laughing.

"You slept in the barn for three days until the fox was trapped and relocated! You were willing to do anything."

"They were fragile and vulnerable. But what does this have to do with the man who murdered Father Myriel?"

"Everything!" Her voice boomed, Eli startled.

"We children of Europe have a problem, an addiction."

"I'm sorry, Sister; I'm not following."

Sister Francis decided to make her point.

"Eli, the way you felt about those rabbits is the way we feel about *ourselves*. We have an incessant need to love and protect the things we hold dear."

"Doesn't everyone and every group of people think they're special?"

"For sure, nothing wrong with that," Sister Francis continued. "But we take it one step further. Not only do we think that we are special, but we also think that . . ." She paused.

Even she struggled with owning what she was about to say next.

"Think what?" Eli needed her to finish.

Francis had reached the point of no return.

"We think you are the fox." Sister Francis looked down as if embarrassed.

"What do you mean?" asked Eli.

"We fear the children of Africa. You threaten our vulnerabilities."

"I don't understand."

"You must be trapped. Controlled. Removed from threatening that which we hold dear. Or else."

"Or else what?" Eli asked.

"Or else. Period."

The teakettle began to whistle.

"How did we get into a conversation about racism?" young Eli challenged. "All I want to know is why that man murdered Father Myriel."

Sister Francis poured the hot water over their tea bags and sat back down.

"Eli, I know that you loved him and that this is hard, but I want to give you the real answer or at least the answer as best as I know it. What happened that day happens every day in our community. If you don't know what it is, then it will get you too."

Eli thought of the irony of a white woman trying to teach him about race.

She broke the silence with a story. "Do you know I used to teach at Gilpin Elementary School in Five Points?"

Eli didn't. He'd only known Sister Francis as Father Myriel's right hand at St. Augustine's. She coordinated the services, organized the daily food service, and kept tabs on the mission's overall operations.

He shook his head.

"Yes, used to teach first grade. It gave me great satisfaction to help them get their all-day sea legs after kindergarten half days. My goal was to instill a good foundation for future success. I loved those kids."

Eli added another log to the fire.

"The first day of class was always a jarring experience."

"What do you mean?" Eli asked.

"First days are always hectic, with kids all stressed about the unknown of new friends and adjusting to the fact that the dog days of summer were now in the rearview mirror. But the hardest part as a teacher was not managing the antsy and anxious kids but navigating the demands of the parents."

Eli had to trust Sister Francis at this point.

She continued, "The parents were worried too. They were reliving their own first-day memories and trying to fix—even in elementary school—all their educational misfortunes and regrets. Some parents . . ."

Young Eli's mind wandered for a moment, not seeing what this had to do with what killed—murdered—the only parent he'd had.

"I'll bet you have some stories," Eli said, hoping that comment was in line with where Francis was in her story.

"For sure, for sure!"

Francis now remembered why she was telling Eli all of this.

"Eli, I was the only white teacher in the school. Gilpin was an all-black school in an all-black neighborhood. I stood out like, well, a white nun at an all-black school!"

She laughed, Eli smiled.

"So here's my point. It never failed that on the first day of school, a black mom would walk her black child into the classroom of one of my black colleagues and then, almost immediately, go to the principal's office."

"Why's that?" Eli asked.

"Because she wanted her child in a different classroom, with a different teacher."

Eli's face let on that he wasn't following.

"These black mothers would go to the black principal's office and demand that their black child be moved to my classroom."

She paused. "Can you believe that? They moved them from the black teacher to me, the white teacher."

Eli was dumbfounded.

"You wanted to know why that man murdered Father Myriel? That's why."

Eli wasn't sure if he wanted the conversation to continue.

"Eli, I'm sorry to ask you to do this," she was speaking with all delicacy. "But I want you to think back to the day Father Myriel died."

He didn't have to try hard; the memory was as present as his breath.

"Eli, what color was the man who murdered Father Myriel?"

While Eli hadn't seen who the man was, he had seen this one detail and shared it with Sister Francis. Eli's mind wouldn't allow him to say the word. Francis had so gently brought him to this moment, and now the enormity of what she was trying to communicate to him came all at once. Centuries of truth, as best as he could understand, fell upon him, suffocating his soul. He lost his breath as he tried to answer her question.

What color was the man who killed my father?

He felt her gaze as his mouth formed the word but withheld any sound.

His lips betrayed his thoughts as Eli spoke just shy of a whisper.

"Black."

Eli stood up, unable to look her in the eye, and left the room.

That was almost twenty years ago, and while Eli still struggled with the reliability of learning about race from a child of Europe, he never forgot Sister Francis's explanation for Father Myriel's murder. One time he told Antoinette, "The biggest problem with America is not white supremacy; it's America's belief in black inferiority."

Today, Eli remembered that conversation as he rode in a taxicab that was following Slager, a black detective, home from the courthouse. Eli knew that Slager had framed at least two men and was convinced that he had done the same to Langston. Why would a black man do this to other black men? How did he start seeing his own, rabbits in need of protection, as foxes that needed to be eliminated?

Eli had spent his life wondering if Slager would come back for him. Now Eli, knowing that he could no longer avoid the truth, stalked the man he'd been hiding from all these years.

JUDGE'S DECISION

Langston watched Liza out of the back window of the armored transport bus.

After the judge's decision, he was whisked out of the courtroom and sent back to the only home he'd known for the past fifteen years.

Liza followed in her hail-dented Toyota Corolla. He wished he'd been there to help her buy her first car. At the time of his arrest, she had been saving, and they had plans to find a deal together.

"Get something reliable when you're young, save flashy for later," he had told her.

She made a good choice without me.

The bus and the Corolla turned west toward Stratling.

She's gonna be all right..

With each mile closer to that forsaken place, Langston watched Liza as she watched him. He could see her tears sparkling in the late day sun as she kept her car closer than was safe to the back of the bus.

With each mile, the judge's words reverberated for both of them with the whine of the tires.

"Motion denied."

That was it. No preamble. No explanation. Just two words.

They'd barely sat down, and then the courtroom was emptied, leaving him with the hollow assurances of his lawyer as they ushered him out, leaving Liza sitting stunned with Elizabeth. Langston wasn't sure where Eli had gone.

They arrived at Stratling, and after making them wait an hour, the guards strip-searched Langston and brought him to Liza, who waited in the visiting room.

"Daddy, we still have time," she blurted. "We have more questions than answers, but we'll figure this out. We are going to come up with something. I am not giving up."

God, take care of my baby.

"Daddy, the project is meeting first thing tomorrow; we'll brainstorm. We'll come up with a plan. There's still time."

Langston knew today had been his last chance, and when the judge didn't allow his attorney a fair shot at discrediting the eyewitness, he knew it was over. Hearing the judge's denial of his motion was not a surprise, just a mere formality.

For all these years, he'd never been able to figure out why he was fingered for the crime and by whom. Whom did he cross? What did he do to end up on the wrong side of the powers that be? Why did they work so hard to pin the case on him?

Langston started to feel as if two large snakes were coiled around and constricting each of his lungs.

"Baby, you have to prepare yourself."

He struggled to get air back into his chest.

The yellowish tint of the lights now felt like a dimming haze surrounding them.

"No, Daddy, you have to keep fighting."

Langston looked up at the window above Liza's head. The bird and nest were both gone.

"Billie," they were holding hands, and the metal table underneath felt extra cold, "you've done an amazing job."

She started to interrupt, but Langston was determined that she hear him out.

"Billie, I love you. I am immensely proud of you. You are an incredible mother. And, as a daughter, I couldn't have asked for more." He was resolute. "You are going to be fine. You will thrive. Just promise me that you'll never forget how much I love you. It has been an honor to be your father."

Before she could argue her case, Langston shouted over his shoulder, "Guard!"

"Daddy, wait."

"I can't. I need to go." He needed to prepare himself.

The guards arrived and removed him as Liza stood, hands covering her mouth.

"Daddy, please. No."

Once out of sight, his knees decided not to hold his weight, but he refused to go down, especially in front of the guards.

When he arrived at his cell, Governor Stash was on his TV announcing that Langston would be next.

Again, Langston had thirty days to live.

LIZA'S DESPAIR

Closing time conversations were now the norm for Eli and Liza, and this was their first chance to catch up since the judge's decision.

Eli poured, and they began to talk. Eli didn't have a drink; he was saving that for Antoinette.

"How's your father?"

"Still trying to be strong. I know he's struggling, but putting on a good face."

They paused as a waitress asked Liza a question from across the room.

Liza then finished her thought. "He's still protecting me, guiding me and being my dad."

"I can't imagine," Eli said, resting both forearms on the bar. "As a dad, he wants to keep you safe from pain. Must be hard for him with so much out of his control."

She nodded.

"And you haven't made it easy," Eli added.

"What do you mean?"

"You've run headlong toward the pain with relentless resolve. All your dad wants is for you to move on, but his case has consumed you."

"More than his case, his freedom. I want my dad back home, my parents to grow old together, my daughter to know her grandfather outside that dark gray dungeon."

Sensing that she was getting defensive, Eli interjected, "Liza, I'm not criticizing you, I'm just saying he's trying to be a good dad to an incredible daughter. He's trying to protect you because he loves you, and because you love him, you refuse to let pain get in the way."

"Thank you."

"You have to admit, you've missed out on a lot. During your twenties, when others are chasing their dreams and putting in a foundation for their future, you were working on your father's freedom."

"It may not be the life I wanted, but it's the life he needed. Plus I got my degree. May not have been Juilliard, but ain't no shame in community college."

"Cheers to that," Eli raised his hand as if it held a glass. "And you're almost finished with your juris doctorate. Pretty impressive."

"Yeah, who says I can't be the singing lawyer?" She tapped her glass against his hand.

Eli wondered what was going to happen to Liza in less than four weeks. After the funeral. What would she do with herself? He thought of Homer and his tragic character Odysseus, who faced his greatest battles trying to find his way back home. Eli knew from personal experience that once you give yourself to a fight, it's hard to see your way back home when the battle is over. He knew that both his and Liza's most significant battles were most likely in front of them.

Eli thought about saying that but decided against it.

"So, what are the lawyers saying?"

The last of the workers had left. They were alone.

"They say that we are out of options and that Mom and I need to prepare for the worst."

"Sorry."

"How can they give up so quickly? He's innocent, and they're an innocence project. They have to do something. He's going to die; they're going to kill Daddy."

Eli handed her a cocktail napkin.

"I just need more time. I know we can find a way to clear his name and get him out of there."

Eli just listened as he admired the tattoo on her chest. It was hard to tell, but it seemed to flow seamlessly under her blouse, peeked out the other side of her short sleeve, and made its way down her right arm. He guessed it probably decorated her back too.

"Did you see the look on that witness's face? That was the look of doubt. She knew she was the guilty one. If that judge just would've let Daddy have the same opportunity as that white cop, then the truth would've come out. She never saw him running that morning. She just saw some black man, and after a little coaxing and help from the police, she told them what they wanted to hear. She knows it. I know it. We all know it."

Silence.

"What's Mom going to do? I can't let this happen."

Eli almost told her about the expiration dates on the death cocktail and how he suspected Duncan's botched execution probably meant that the drugs were already past legal usage. But he had no proof. Telling her would only increase her torment and give false hope.

"Time. We need a little more time. If only the governor would—" she stopped herself. "And tell me, why is Governor Stash pushing all of this? I know he wants to get reelected, but seems like something else is behind all of this."

Eli now had Slager's address.

"Could you use some time off over the next month or so?" Eli offered, trying not to imply that Langston was going to die. "We can manage around here."

Eli knew that he needed to do something.

"No, yeah . . . I don't know," Liza said.

Eli then decided to ask her a direct, blunt question. "Liza, is there any realistic hope for your father?"

Eli watched Liza search her mind. It was as if she were rereading every transcript, sorting through every piece of evidence, and replaying every moment of testimony.

She didn't say anything, but the answer was clear to both of them.

Her silence confirmed it.

Eli must confront the one man who could save Langston's life.

Slager.

(Twenty-eight days to live)

ASCENT

It was 2 AM, and Eli was standing in the alley across the street from one of Denver's high-rise apartment buildings just a couple of blocks from the 16th Street Mall. As he looked up, he could see the dim glow of light in one of the twentieth-floor apartments.

Slager was awake.

Eli crossed the street and opened the large glass doors leading into the lobby. He was surprised not to find a concierge at the desk or a night-time attendant snoozing in his chair. Still, he was cognizant of potential security cameras, so he kept his head down and his hat low, hiding his face.

The lobby was posh. Polished granite floors reflected the chandelier lights. Eli studied his face in them as he walked, head down. On his left was a spacious seating area like that of an upscale hotel lobby. Couches and tables provided workspace and gathering areas. Two fireplaces framed the room, and in the back corner there was a door that led to a private theater room.

How does a city detective afford to live in a place like this?

Eli made his way to the bank of elevators, and after filling his chest with air, he pressed the elevator button. He could hear the low din of the gears as they summoned the mirrored carriage from the floors above. Eli, still trying to hide his face, peeked out from beneath the brim of his hat to check his reflection in the brushed-silver doors.

At the sight of himself, doubt crept close, and he was even more unsure of his plan than when he was outside looking up at Slager's window.

When the doors slid open, Eli was grateful to find the elevator empty. He pressed the button and the doors closed; his stomach signaled that the twenty-floor climb had begun.

I hope he doesn't call the police. He is the police, will he arrest me? Worse?

He hoped that he could appeal to the humanity he'd witnessed as he crouched outside the confessional so many years ago. There'd been a glimmer of a man who knew right from wrong. He'd confessed to a priest for a reason. While Eli believed Slager had murdered Father Myriel, there was a moment when he'd considered a different path. Eli hoped to help him see that path again.

The gears accelerated.

Eli fingered the beads on his bracelet.

Kyrie Eleison.

The elevator came to a stop, and the doors opened like the curtain to a Broadway show, revealing an entryway with a wrought-iron chandelier suspended from the high ceiling. Cherrywood floors prepared to meet his feet as he stepped out into the hallway.

Six residences occupied this floor. Slager resided in a prime corner apartment with a view of Pikes Peak. Eli had discovered this after asking Fredricka for another favor.

"You already owe me, Mr. Stone. Are you sure you want to increase your debt to me?"

Eli turned to the right.

Lifted his head high.

You should have done this a long time ago. For Father Myriel. For Langston. For Liza. No turning back.

WHISKEY NIGHTS

Slager sat and swirled his whiskey.

After the judge's decision, he was satisfied that his sins would end up buried with Langston and the others he'd put on death row.

For years he'd feared that his past would catch up. It only seemed like a matter of time before someone, somewhere, came forward, forcing him to answer for his many misdeeds.

In his mind, though, he'd reached the point long ago of seeing his wrongs as rights on behalf of his community, his people. "To Serve and Protect" was his mantra when he took his oath as a young officer, and as far as he was concerned, he'd never wavered from that ideal.

"It's not easy to serve and protect when the handcuffs are on the good guys," he wrote in one of his many journals. He fancied himself a writer of sorts. In retirement, he planned to run off to Mexico and churn out pulp fiction based on his real-life experiences. A book every couple of years should be enough to pay his cerveza tab each night.

He would write for money and his soul.

Deep down he knew that he had sins to atone for and that confession was in his future, but for now, he was convinced that the ends had justified his means. All the people he'd arrested, framed, and lied about knew in their heart of hearts that they were guilty of something, somewhere, at some time.

He already had the opening line of his first book, *Concrete Jungle*, "If you shoot a lion for eating a gazelle, it doesn't matter when you do it because you know, given the nature of the animal, at some time it had blood on its jowls."

Slager's late grandmother, Mema, once left a bingo game only to have two black teens hit her from behind. One, like a linebacker, knocked her onto the hood of a car, while the other snagged her purse like a cornerback in need of a new contract. Slager remembered her coming home with bloody scraped knees and a bruised heart for having to identify two neighbor boys who lived down the block. Mema agonized, Slager fumed. "Grandma, when I'm grown, I'll protect you. You'll never have to be afraid."

For Slager, it was that simple. "There needs to be a talented few who serve and protect the masses. If that means a few of our own need culling from the herd, so be it," he wrote.

He wasn't proud of his work, but he was convinced that his willingness to do what needed to be done produced a neighborhood that would be safe for the Memas of the world. He reasoned that Five Points was safer because he had dared to face the lions.

The knock at his door woke him from his daze.

Putting down his whiskey, he opened the door mostly expecting to see the face of one of his neighbors apologizing for disturbing him so late.

The last person he expected to see was a priest.

SLAGER'S RECKONING

On Eli's twenty-first birthday, Sister Francis gave him Father Myriel's hat, cane, and clerical collar. Along with the books, they were among the few possessions that he kept after Antoinette's death.

He wore them to confront Slager, not so much to shock him but to remind him of who he was and of the power of truth. Eli hoped that Slager would remember the words that Father Myriel spoke to him so many years ago in the confessional: "My son, you have to make this right."

After knocking, Eli tried to swallow his pulse. As he heard Slager's footsteps, he thought about running; the slide and click of the deadbolt signaled that it was too late to turn back.

When the door opened, Eli was surprised to see Slager still dressed for work, including his shoes but minus his coat and tie. His face didn't let on what he was thinking, though, and both men stared, waiting for the other to speak first.

Eli wasn't sure if the detective recognized the hat and cane as the very ones that had belonged to Father Myriel.

Slager broke the silence. "May I . . . I mean, Father, how may I help you?"

Eli leaned on the cane and peered into the cluttered apartment. The entryway hardwood needed sweeping, and by the looks of the carpet, the vacuum required repair.

Slager had a moment of clarity. "Aren't you, I mean, Father, aren't you the gentleman who sits with Brown's daughter in the courtroom? I . . . I didn't know you were a priest."

Still not sure if this was a good idea, Eli ventured, "Detective, before it's too late, I've come with the hope that you will allow me to help you clean up the mess you've made."

"Have we met before?" asked Slager.

Eli decided to commit. "You don't know me, but I know you."

Eli noticed that Slager instinctively moved his right hand to where his gun usually rested in his shoulder holster. He was thankful it wasn't there.

"I knew you before all of this." Eli stepped forward, and Slager stepped back, as if the moves were choreographed.

Neither knew who closed the door.

"I was there."

Eli's eyes were now taking in extra light as his adrenaline spiked even higher.

He waited as Slager frantically flipped through the Rolodex of his mind, searching for a name, for a handle that would help him grasp what he was dealing with. Was this the husband of one of his many trysts? Had he arrested this man? Roughed him up as a beat cop?

"I intend you no harm." Eli sensed his fear.

Slager tried to take control. "Harm? Why would you think that I would feel threatened by a priest? Forgive my manners, may I get you something to drink? Tea, water—"

"Whiskey."

Eli smelled it on Slager's breath and felt the need for some liquid courage.

"Alrighty, Father, whiskey it is."

Eli sat in the dusty leather chair across from the well-worn recliner with remote and Jack Daniels on flanking side tables. Slager retrieved another glass. Eli watched to see if he also picked up some protection along the way.

Slager sat and poured two fingers for himself, one for Eli.

"My apologies for such a late and unannounced visit."

Eli tried to steer the conversation back on track.

"No problem, Father, no problem," Slager replied, still unsure. "You said you've come to help me clean up a mess. I'm not quite sure what you are referring to, but I'm always willing to listen to a man of the cloth. I once knew—"

"Detective Slager," Eli was now focused. "Let's not be coy."

"Father, I don't know what—"

"I was there," Eli blurted.

"Beg your pardon?"

"I was there. The afternoon Father Myriel was murdered. I heard everything you confessed."

Again Slager felt for his gun.

"Detective, I'm sorry."

Slager was silent.

Eli tried to give him space to process what was happening. After all, Eli was dressed as a priest and had just said that he was there the day Father Myriel was murdered, that he had heard what was said in the confessional.

Slager must have thought that his admission of misdeeds died with Father Myriel, but now this priest had shown up unannounced in the middle of the night, jarring his illusion of untouchability.

"I'm sorry," Eli repeated. "I was there on that day all those years ago when you made your last confession to Father Myriel. I hid behind the cabinet next to the confessional."

"Wait, I know who you are. You're that kid, Father Myriel's acolyte, who used to go everywhere with him."

"Yes. And you might remember that after the service, when you asked to speak with Father, he sent me away. But instead of leaving, I hid. I knew it was wrong, but it was just something I did. Hearing grown folk talk about their problems made me feel better about mine. If they hadn't figured out life, then maybe there was hope for me."

Eli waited as Slager poured another round.

"So when you, a police officer, came in that day, I knew I had to hear what you were going to say. There was no way I was going to miss out on your secrets."

Eli apologized again, then continued.

"I heard everything." He paused to allow the gravity of that statement to settle. Slager lit a cigarette.

"I was crushed. I looked up to you, all of us neighborhood kids did. You were a black man wearing blue. You were one of us, protecting us from the worst among us, but you betrayed us by—"

"I did no such thing," Slager said with a volume meant to convince his own ears.

Eli wanted to challenge that assertion instead. "Forgive me, I didn't come here to condemn you. I came here to help."

"Listen, Father, I don't know what you think you know, but perhaps it's best that you leave. You are mistaken about what happened."

Eli decided to come clean. "I'm not a priest. I'm far from the good man that Father Myriel was. This hat," Eli then pointed to the collar, "all of this was his. I wore it hoping that you might remember—"

"Remember what? I told you I wasn't there."

"Detective, I was there. I saw you through the slats, your countenance, the brown leather notebook that you read from. I heard everything."

Slager looked at him, stone-faced.

"I remember exactly what you said." Eli quoted Slager verbatim, "Father, I have sinned . . . I've framed a man."

Eli pressed on, "Dontel. You framed Dontel."

"Dontel was the thug of thugs, a criminal."

"I came here to help you."

"Detective, do you remember the last words Father Myriel spoke to you?"

Slager didn't react.

"Father said, 'My son, you have to make this right. God forgives, and so do I, but you need to let me help you.'"

DESCENT

"Let me help you." Eli's offer pierced the silence.

Slager sat stoic-eyed.

"I know you're afraid. The human spirit wasn't meant to hold secrets. My brother, let me help you."

Eli assumed that Slager was looking for a way out.

He must have rehearsed this moment before. He'd probably practiced his alibi for each of his indiscretions and fooled himself into thinking that he'd be able to bluff Internal Affairs or a jury of police-friendly citizens predisposed to believe in his truthfulness.

But now his rehearsals failed him.

Slager remained silent.

"You can stop this," Eli continued. "No one else needs to die. You're trying to cover your tracks with the blood of those you're convinced are guilty of something even if it's not what you put them away for.

"And what if you were wrong? Are you so sure that all of them were guilty?" Langston was entirely on Eli's mind.

"I can't . . ." Slager didn't finish.

"Are you positive that Langston Brown is guilty? He didn't have a criminal record. His wife and daughter support his alibi of being at home, celebrating Mother's Day. Are you sure?"

Eli knew that Slager must have considered what would happen to him if he went to prison. Police officers didn't fare well there regardless of the reason they were locked up, but him, every day he'd face people he'd framed. His life would be a nightmare. On top of that, Eli wanted to confront Slager with the murder of Myriel, but he wasn't sure what the reaction would be, so he stuck with the most imminent.

"Langston is innocent, and you can save his life. He has a wife and daughter. His granddaughter has never seen him outside of Stratling."

Slager finally spoke, "What do you want me to do?"

Eli wasn't expecting to get this far. Slager's words were akin to an admission.

He just started talking, "You don't have to tell everything, at least not yet. You could start by saving Langston Brown's life if you just shared your own doubts about Langston with the judge." Eli thought of Fredricka and her team. "Or maybe we could keep your name out of it. I know a journalist; you could tell her, and she could tell the city."

Eli was grasping at straws.

"They'd eventually find out. My life would be over."

Eli continued to offer options.

Slager looked out the window.

Snow was falling.

* * *

"Do you think God forgives?" Slager changed the subject.

Both men knew the answer. They'd heard Father Myriel speak about God's love on many occasions.

"God loves you, and there's nothing you can do about it!" was one of his oft-repeated refrains.

Myriel would ask, "Do you know the most prayed prayer in the scriptures?"

The congregation would respond in unison, "Lord, have mercy."

"That's right—Kyrie Eleison. He's a merciful God."

"I think we both know the answer to that," Eli responded. The irony that Eli wore Myriel's uniform was not lost on either of them.

"I need to know. That's why I asked to see Father Myriel that day. I was there to confess my sins, to find forgiveness, but all he wanted was justice. All he wanted to talk about was how I could—should—make things right. That was not why I was there."

Slager's voice quaked. Eli was unsure if he was sensing anger or fear.

"All I wanted to know was if God would forgive me."

"Do you believe that you did wrong?" Eli asked.

"Hell no!" Slager's eyes bulged. "Those thugs were ruining everything. I did what I had to do to stop them. I fulfilled my vow to serve and protect my community, my people. And if some self-righteous, collar-wearing Negro doesn't like it, then you can—"

"What about what you did to Father Myriel? You don't think that was wrong? You murdered my father. You may deny that the others were innocent, but you can't go call him a thug. He was a good man, and yet you took his life.

"Man, what are you talking about?"

"You came back to silence the one person who knew your secrets. Brother—"

"Would you stop calling me your brother! If I were, then you wouldn't be here trying to get me to put myself behind bars."

"My brother, I was there. I heard what you said. I know what you did. What you gonna do now, huh? Gonna kill me too? When does it stop?"

Eli immediately regretted letting his anger steer them into treacherous territory. "OK, never mind, let's go back to what you were saying. If you don't think you've done anything wrong, then why do you want to know if you can be forgiven? Forgiven for what?"

Slager glared, side-eyed. Eli froze. He briefly felt like he had that fateful day right before the man seated in front of him had reached through the confessional curtain and grabbed Myriel by the neck.

"Brown. Let's just talk about Langston Brown. You can save an innocent man's life. Make amends . . ."

Eli looked around, searching for a hint as to where the detective's gun might be.

He wouldn't shoot me, would he?

Eli returned to the unanswered question he'd posed a minute before. "Detective, if you don't think you did anything wrong, then why would you need forgiveness?

Slager sat up straight with a purpose.

"Not for what I've done, but for what I'm about to do."

* * *

"You shouldn't have come here." Slager asserted. "I don't know what you'd hoped to accomplish, but I'm afraid you're going to be disappointed."

Eli held his hands up, palms forward, a gesture of nonconfrontation.

"You show up here, wearing his hat and collar, I don't know what you want, but I'm not going to give it to you." The floor creaked as Slager leaned forward on his toes. "And you, I don't care if you were just a kid, how dare you do what you did? Invading the privacy of a moment like that. You, you ought to be ashamed."

Eli nodded as he stared at the large cherrywood bookshelf, contemplating whether he should reply or not.

"Whatever you think you heard, you're wrong. I didn't admit to nothing."

Slager then seemed to realize that the point of a confession was to admit wrongdoing. "Not anything you say I admitted to, nothing you were supposed to hear."

Slager began to ease back into the chair. Eli relaxed.

"I was a good cop. Not perfect, but I was one of the good ones."

Eli noticed the past tense.

"I used to give people second chances and kick 'em breaks, but they didn't care. They'd spit in my face the next time I saw them and called me an Uncle Tom."

Pointing his finger, "Do you know what that feels like? To be rejected by your own? Well, they can all go to hell for all I care. I ain't and never was no Uncle Tom!"

Eli felt like he needed to say something. "I don't think—"

"I chose the night shift for a reason. Had enough seniority to work the plush morning gig, helping old ladies cross the street and sitting in the school zone to keep the small ones safe, but I chose the night, 'cuz that's where I thought I could make a difference. Thought that if our wayward young black men could see me then maybe they'd want to be like me. But what thanks do I get? Names . . . Black Honky, Ebony Cracker . . ."

Slager's right leg was involuntarily shaking; pressure rested on the ball of his foot.

"So don't think that collar you've got on is going to turn me somehow, make me feel all sentimental and spill the proverbial beans. You—"

Eli jumped in, "I'm not here to say you're a bad cop, but I do know what I heard and what I saw, you killed . . ."

Eli fought to find his bearings. "Langston. The point is Langston Brown."

Slager stood up.

"I know about the death cocktail and the expiration dates,"

"I'm not gonna—"

"An innocent man is going to die if you don't tell the truth."

Slager took three long strides and slid open the balcony door. Large snowflakes fell in the windless night. He stepped out.

"Innocent? They're all guilty of something. I just had the guts to get them off the streets by any means necessary."

"Father Myriel, what was he guilty of?" Eli retorted.

Eli watched, not sure what Slager was about to do next.

"Why don't you come back in. Your neighbors can hear you."

"I don't care what they hear. They're able to sleep at night because of me, because I did my job. Do you hear that?"

Slager moved to the rail, left hip touching, and made a sweeping motion with his arm.

"That's right, you don't hear a thing, not one siren is waking anybody up tonight because I did my job. I took every one of those thugs off the street so the city could sleep."

It happened so fast. Eli was helpless.

Slager slung his right leg over the rail, and the left followed. He perched on his toes on the outside edge of the balcony, facing toward the apartment, his back to the open sky. His fingers gripped the rail hard, knuckles pale.

Eli raced to the door, "Detective, don't!" If he let go, then Langston had no chance.

"Don't move."

Slager held up one hand, and then the other.

Eli lunged as Slager floated backward into the night.

(Twenty-seven days to live)

MAN HUNT

The morning news led with the Slager story.

Denver's beloved officer was dead.

"He landed in front of me," said a taxi driver in a live, on-the-scene interview. "Barely missed my car."

"I got out and ran over to him," he continued at the urging of the television reporter. "It was horrible. I've never seen anything like that before."

"What else did you see?"

"Blood. Red everywhere. He wasn't breathing."

The reporter continued, "How terrifying to have witnessed someone committing suicide. We are so sorry for—"

The taxi driver interrupted, "Oh, no, this was no suicide."

"What do you mean?"

"Like I told the police, I looked up, and there was only one apartment with its lights on, and at first it was hard to make out, but there was a person on the balcony looking down on me . . . on us."

"Were you able to describe him to the police?"

"Yes, absolutely, yes."

"What did you tell them?"

"A priest. I saw a black priest."

That evening, as the musicians took a break from performing, all who sat at the bar were glued to the TV.

The Roz was abuzz over Slager's death, Liza especially.

"I can't believe it!" She was standing behind the bar with Eli.

"I don't know what to think, but first of all, he was guilty as hell, so it would make sense that he'd kill himself. But who was that mysterious black priest?"

"We needed him alive," Liza lamented. "He was our last hope . . . he knew more than he let on. If only we could've got him to talk, then maybe we could've saved Daddy."

Eli's mind replayed Slager's suicide in slow motion. He was shaking as he poured a drink for a customer.

"Look." Liza pointed at the news and turned up the volume.

A middle-aged white couple were being interviewed. "We saw him," they calmly told the camera.

Eli froze.

He had left Slager's apartment as quickly as he could. He thought about taking the stairs but opted for the same elevator he had used on his arrival. When the doors opened onto Slager's floor, Eli was face-to-face with the two people who were now on the television. They exited as Eli entered, pressing the close-door button even before he selected the button for the lobby.

"Yes, we saw him getting into the elevator. We know almost everyone in the building, so it did seem odd to us that there was a priest in the building, especially at such a late hour," the man said.

The woman interjected, "We didn't feel the need to call the police or anything. After all, he was a priest."

"What else can you tell us about him?"

"Well, he was a black man of average height, and, oh, he had a cane in one hand and, a bag."

"A suitcase," the man added.

"Yeah, a suitcase in his other hand."

Eli looked at Liza. Liza wanted to talk. Eli needed to go. So he left.

Tonight there was no date with Antoinette.

The hatch slammed as he made his way down the ladder.

Eli was afraid. Three people had seen him. One from afar, two up close, face-to-face. How would he explain?

He thought about Father Burleson. Seeing as he was the only real black priest in Denver, the police must already have him at the station.

The interrogation would be intense.

Would there be a sketch released? That couple must have given a detailed description. It was only a matter of time before the police knocked on his door.

Eli clicked the nob on the record player, and Miles began the serenade.

This time, however, there was no tilting of shelves, no crashing of books. Instead, Eli eyed the suitcase sitting on his cot. Eventually he moved to it and unzipped it. He opened it and removed a brown leather journal. A journal just like the one Slager had with him in the confessional with Father Myriel.

Eli began to read.

(Twenty-six days to live)

PART III

What happens to a dream deferred?
Does it dry up
like a raisin in the sun?
Or fester like a sore—
And then run?
Does it stink like rotten meat?
Or crust and sugar over—
like a syrupy sweet?

Maybe it just sags
like a heavy load.
Or does it explode?
—Langston Hughes

WHAT ABOUT DNA?

"Why can't we do that too?"

Liza was sitting across the desk of her law professor, the director of Project Joseph.

A tall curly-haired man with brown eyes that matched his sweater, Garrett McConnell was a pioneer in what was becoming known as the innocence world.

"Three percent" was a stat he often quoted. "Three percent of all convictions in the United States are wrong. Now we can pat ourselves on the back because we get things right ninety-seven percent of the time or we can face the reality that three percent equals thousands of men and women who are doing time for crimes they didn't commit."

He was stalwart in his mission, but even he had thrown in the towel after the judge's verdict against Langston.

Liza, on the other hand, was far from waving the white flag.

"You need to prepare yourself; we've done our best. Liza, you have fought hard for your father's freedom, but as hard as it is to hear, this is what passes for justice in America. I know you don't want to believe what I'm saying, and I'm sorry to be so blunt, but there are no other options available for your father."

"But what about DNA testing?"

After a high-profile case that involved a former professional football player, DNA was the latest hope for those who found themselves in need of scientific proof of their innocence.

"C'mon," she said as she threw a recent law review article on the table in front of Garrett. "Don't you believe what you wrote?"

Liza picked the paper back up and began to read it aloud.

"America watched as the new science of testing the basic building blocks of biology were put on trial. The consensus was that the NFL star was guilty; the prosecution even presented DNA evidence that placed him at the bloody scene of the crime. But thanks to an all-star team of lawyers, the public received a PhD-level course on the ins and outs of this new biological fingerprint."

She peered at her professor over the top of the paper before continuing.

"DNA is a game changer for people who are truly innocent. While it appears that the famous athlete was able to get away with murder, despite the DNA evidence, we in the innocence world must tout this new science as a premier tool for law enforcement and justice. There will be and should be a long queue of defendants lining up to get their cheeks swabbed with the hope that they might be exonerated. We must see to it that this cutting-edge science gets applied on behalf of those who truly deserve it."

Liza looked at Professor McConnell, pleading with her eyes.

"I believe that day is coming, but we are not there yet. It's such a new procedure, Denver still doesn't have a lab for the testing; we'd have to send it to Chicago. It's a long shot."

"It may be, but it's a shot nonetheless, and we can't afford to leave any bullets in the proverbial chamber."

"What do you propose?"

"Test the bloody shirt!"

A bloody shirt was an unanswered puzzle from Langston's trial. After performing a basic blood type analysis on a shirt worn by one of the dead security guards, it was discovered to have contained two types of blood—one belonging to the deceased guard and the other unmatched, belonging to an unknown person who bled at the scene of the crime. Langston's defense speculated that there was a scuffle in which the real murderer suffered a wound, leaving his blood behind. The prosecution explained this away, but, Liza reasoned, if Project Joseph could test the DNA of the unknown blood sample, it would be clear that it didn't belong to her father.

"The test would prove that the blood of the perpetrator doesn't match Daddy's blood."

Her professor listened.

"We could petition the judge."

"We have no more legal recourse," her professor reminded.

"We could go straight to the governor."

"There's no way we could get an audience."

"We could make our case in the court of public opinion. If it was good enough for that football player, it's good enough for Langston Brown."

"Keep this up, and you'll end up the director of Project Joseph someday," her professor smiled.

Liza loved that idea. On her last birthday, after she blew out the candles, Journey remarked, "Momma, I know what you wished for."

"What's that?"

"You wished for Grandpa to come home."

"Baby girl, that's what I pray for, but I wished for something different."

That night, as Liza tucked Journey into bed, she asked, "So Momma, what did you wish for?"

It was then that Liza voiced the desire of her heart. She told Journey that she wished she could sing again, and when this nightmare had passed and Grandpa was home, Liza hoped that she'd be able to help the other three percent. Running the innocence project was not beyond her dreams.

"Suppose you can get the governor's approval, thus bypassing our lack of appeals. Then what? How would we pay for the test?"

Liza didn't know the answer. What she did know was that time was not slowing down for her father.

(Twenty-five days to live)

FOR BETTER OR FOR WORSE

Inevitable silence filled the space between them.

Langston and Elizabeth reminisced without words.

Over the years the visiting room at Stratling Correctional Facility had become their living room.

It was here that she updated him on Liza, filled him in on the latest goings-on in Five Points, and tried to keep her husband's spirits bolstered for the battle.

Langston remembered his line about how they met: "I settled down in Denver 'cuz I found a woman who settled for me!"

They met on the sidewalk outside Shorter AME Church. Elizabeth was on her way into the Wednesday night prayer meeting and Langston, though he was really on his way to the basketball court, decided that he was up for some praying too.

He was thankful the church didn't care how you dressed on Wednesday night.

"Save your Sunday clothes for Sunday. On Wednesday, just come as you are," the pastor would say, recognizing that most of his people would be even later if they had to run home to change out of their work overalls and kitchen aprons.

After a little bit of whoopin' and hollerin' and a whole lot of praying, Langston summoned the courage to ask Elizabeth out.

On their first date, Langston sped Elizabeth home, running red lights. He was hell-bent on having her on her parents porch before her father's curfew. That night they weren't late, or even on time; Langston had her out of the car and walking through the door fifteen minutes early to ensure there would be no reason they couldn't have a second date.

"We were in love even before our hearts were aware," Elizabeth would say every anniversary as she rested in his embrace.

Langston would register his rebuttal.

"I knew I loved you on that sidewalk outside the church. What do you think I was praying for that night?"

They would laugh, and little Liza would shout from her makeshift bed in the living room, "You know I can hear you guys," causing them all to break out in laughter.

Langston was tall and always bear-like in stature and voice. Elizabeth was small but strong in attitude and sass.

Life together was an easy struggle to pay the bills and raise little Liza. Three jobs between them were the norm, but they always seemed to find time to be with and present for each other.

Now they sat, thirty-five years after they promised that they'd be together no matter what. Back then they had no idea of the nightmare that would come their way.

The hardest part of the past decade and a half was not the shame of Langston's conviction nor the bankrupting legal battle; those things were nothing compared to their longing to be together again. To not have their husband-and-wife moments interrupted with the guard's call of "Time's up."

Langston thought of the last night they spent in the same bed together. Tired as they were, they caught up on the day. Langston shared stories from the shop; Elizabeth talked about Liza. Both, as they drifted off to sleep, dreamed about revolution. If they had known what the next day held, they would have made love one last time.

Now they sit, knowing they are close to their last everything together. In a few weeks, what God had joined together would be violently separated.

So they reminisced in silence, waiting for their last, last call.

Langston wanted to tell her that she's been his rock. He knew that she wanted to remind him to be strong, but to speak would be to acknowledge more than their hearts could handle.

For now, they looked into each other's aged eyes with the same love they brought to the church altar so many years before, a love tested by the worst the world had to offer, a love that had proved true.

Finally, Elizabeth whispered through quivering lips, "I do."

Langston mustered a strong but faint sound, "You did."

THE JOURNALS

Eli had lunged toward Slager when the detective let go of his balcony and fell into the night. He was too late to grab hold of the plunging man but not too late for these two men—both loved by Father Myriel—to communicate one last time.

Slager looked up at Eli and didn't blink until his body collided with the concrete below. Eli wished he'd closed his eyes at that moment instead of watching Slager to the end.

Eli leaned on the railing and lamented not so much for Slager but for the loss of what he thought was his last chance to free both Langston and Liza and make things right for countless others. He felt responsible because he had pushed Slager about the murder of Father Myriel.

When Eli knocked on Slager's door, he'd hoped that somehow Slager would confess or, at the very least, give him something that he could take back to Liza. Slager arresting him was the worst-case scenario that he'd imagined. He'd never considered the possibility that he'd be looking down on Slager's lifeless body, now with people gathering around.

As one of them looked up and pointed, Eli backed away from the railing and stepped back into the apartment, but then he stopped cold.

Right before Slager let go of the railing, Eli's eyes locked on Slager's, but Slager wasn't looking at Eli. He was instead looking at something behind Eli. Now as Eli looked into the apartment's living room, he saw what Slager was looking at.

Eli stood before a large, ornate cherrywood bookshelf that he had glanced at a few times during his conversation with Slager. He recognized most of the titles it held, but mostly he noticed their lack of order. Some of the books sat with the lettering on the bindings facing right, while others faced left. This bothered Eli as much as misaligned bottles behind a bar. If he had been there on more friendly terms with Slager, he would have tidied the disorder for reasons of his own sanity.

Was Slager—consciously or unconsciously—giving him a clue or trying to catch his eye? Eli didn't know. What he did know was that now he could see the bottom shelf that had previously been blocked from his view by Slager's chair.

It was a shelf of brown journals, each one identical to the journal Slager had read in the confessional as Eli eavesdropped. There were a dozen or more sitting in the spot where Slager looked before he let go.

Eli gathered them all and stuffed them into a suitcase that he found in the foyer closet.

* * *

The significance of the journals immediately became clear when Eli began to flip through them back in his home. In these volumes, Slager kept candid notes of his exploits.

The journals read in part like a confession. Was he saving them for a final deathbed moment of contrition? Eli even found the page that Slager read to Father Myriel, "Father, I have sinned . . . I've framed a man. "

But they weren't all confessional in nature. Mostly they read like bad first drafts of detective novels. To Eli, it seemed that Slager had a vivid imagination and had planned a future writing career. However, some of the stories felt strangely familiar, oddly true.

The night that Eli brought them home and dropped them down the portal to his underground library, he read Slager's story titled "The Panel Truck Rapist." It was a story of a black man who preyed on young black women. His MO was to park his panel truck next to their cars in the parking lots of restaurants and bars in order to ambush them when they returned to their vehicles. In the story, a heroic black detective suspected a man from the neighborhood who owned a similar truck. This detective was never able to catch the man in the act, but he planted evidence to get an arrest and a conviction.

"The ends justify the means" was the final line of the story.

Was this story about Duncan, the man who recently died with fire in his veins? Was he innocent? Did Slager frame him too?

Whatever Slager's reason was for keeping the journals, Eli discovered names, places, bits of dialogue, locations, and a seemingly fictional detective who protected his people "By Any Means Necessary," as one of the titles stated.

Over the past week, these journals replaced Eli's preferred evening reading.

One night, as he reached the end of another one of Slager's tales and turned the page, he found written in the top margin, "LANGSTON BROWN."

Underneath was Langston's home address and a line that read "Working Title: The Mother's Day Massacre."

Then Eli read the following cryptic riddle: "Beneath the dormant stench of death it lies."

HYPOTHETICALLY SPEAKING

Eli closed the door to the corner office, drowning out the sound of the morning pool of reporters as they chased tips and would-be headlines. They felt the pressure of competing with the city's two mega-papers. *The Weekly Word* didn't have all the bells and whistles, no sports page or even weather coverage. Fredricka pressured them to do more with less. What they had was grit.

Led by their star investigative reporter, Roberta Messay, they covered city hall like the morning fog over the lake at City Park. Nothing got past them.

"She digs until she hits bedrock or the mother lode," Fredricka was fond of saying.

Eli sat down on the couch. Fredricka stood and unbuttoned the top of her blouse.

"How's it going with Mrs. Messay, any progress?"

Eli had called ahead to say he was on his way. He usually just appeared, but he hoped the call would let her know that this wasn't a social visit.

"Eli, you can't just stroll in here and think we're just gonna talk business and nothing else."

Eli didn't react.

Fredricka removed her shoes and sat in her usual, middle-cushion spot, close enough to touch him.

"I'll say it once so we can move on. You know I'm here for you, and don't forget that you owe me."

She paused just long enough for him to know she was serious, then started a new line of thought.

"We're facing some pretty strong headwinds; no one's talking. It's like they've learned their lesson. My guess is that no one's talking because no one knows anything. It appears the governor's kept a pretty tight circle."

"Freddy, I know you. You don't put all your eggs in one nest. Outside of looking for loose lips, what other angles are you working?"

"Germany. There aren't many companies that make the drugs used in the death cocktail, so we're going straight to the source. We have a reporter on the way as we speak."

Eli nodded for her to continue.

"I don't have much more. We're working on it, but these things take time. Eli, why are you pressing so hard on this? This is unusual for you. In the past, you've shown interest in our stories mostly out of curiosity, but nothing like this."

Eli kept it going. "Can't you at least publish an article that outlines your suspicions? If the public knew your suspicions, then you might be able to slow things down. Freddy, you have to do something."

"It's her, isn't it?" turning the tables.

"Who?"

"You know who."

Eli said nothing.

"I'd always hoped it would be me, but I understand."

Still nothing.

"It's OK. Tell me about her."

"Liza's not the reason I'm here. There's nothing between us. She doesn't even know about the expired drugs; that would devastate her even more. All she knows is that her father is about to be executed for a crime that we, including you, don't believe he committed. Freddy, he has less than three weeks to live!"

Eli's heart was still tender.

"I know how much you loved Antoinette. I could only hope to be loved half as much someday. You must miss her terribly."

Eli was grateful that she decided not to press the point and took the opportunity to change the subject.

"What do you hear about Slager?"

"That no one wants to believe that Denver's favorite black son committed suicide, and when they catch that black priest, he has some explaining to do, that's what I'm hearing."

"Do they have any suspects?"

"After interrogating poor Father Burleson, they discovered an air-tight alibi."

"What was that?"

"He was in Rome. The Vatican of all places. Having the pope vouch for your whereabouts is about as good as it gets."

"Who else are they looking at?"

"Not hearing about anyone in particular except that they're increasing the number of detectives assigned to the case and having that couple sit down with a sketch artist. I wouldn't be surprised if they held a big press conference soon announcing a special task force with reward money to chum the waters."

Eli stared at the light reflecting off her fingernails; the ceiling fan made shadows in the red gloss. She ran them through her beach blond hair. He vacillated between admiration of her competence and indecision over whether or not he should tell her what he knew.

"Freddy, I have a question."

"Go ahead. I've been waiting for you to get to the real reason for your visit."

"What if Slager left something behind?"

"Like what?"

"Like evidence or something."

"What are you saying?"

"I'm saying," Eli measured his words, "Slager wasn't murdered."

"Go on."

"I'm saying that I know things, nothing solid, but I'm on to something that could shake up the whole city, even take down the governor. And—if we can figure this out—we'll save Langston's life."

Eli was standing now, and he knew what Fredricka was going to ask next. She was too good a journalist to let this moment pass.

"It was you, wasn't it? You were there that night, on the balcony, weren't you?"

Eli said nothing, knowing that his silence was her confirmation.

"Mr. Stone, you better watch your back."

* * *

As Eli stepped out onto the sidewalk, the air was calm and the sun was bright.

To his left, a parked police car with two officers inside blocked his way back to Five Points.

He turned right and headed south on Broadway.

Eli didn't know the RTD bus system well enough to find an alternate route, so he scanned the street for a taxi but then remembered that it was illegal in Denver for cabs to pick up a waving person on the side of the road. He needed to get back to Five Points before a panic attack set in.

Two young mothers walked toward him pushing double-wide strollers; he made way for them, dodging the parking meters that dotted the edge of the sidewalk.

He dared not look back to see if the police were out of their car, following.

Fredricka's final words echoed, "You better watch your back."

He crossed the street, jaywalking.

If she knew something, she would have told me.

Still headed away from home.

What if they're on to me? There were witnesses who saw me up close.

Eli passed two men standing still, smoking cigarettes. Another man, separated from the first two by a short distance, stood doing nothing.

Undercover.

Eli crossed Eighth Street, one block from Spear Boulevard.

He spotted another man doing nothing and altered his course again, turning left, away from the distant mountains, down an alleyway.

He could smell last night's discarded leftovers as he passed the dumpster for a Vietnamese restaurant.

Alley. Street. Alley.

He risked a look behind and, seeing no one, crossed behind a record store and comic book shop.

What if they already know who I am?

There wasn't a concierge in the lobby of Slager's building, but what about security cameras? Was he recorded as he entered, rode the elevator? He'd tried to keep his face down, but would grainy security footage appear on the evening news, sparking a citywide search?

It's only a matter of time before they find me. I must have left something behind.

Eli took inventory and remembered placing the cane and hat inside the door as usual.

Fingerprints?

Fredricka had made sure that Eli's photo filled a quarter page next to the five-star review of The Roz's opening night.

The couple from the elevator, what if they saw the picture?

Eli made sure his head was down now. No one was going to catch a glimpse.

The retail shops gave way to boutique apartment buildings along Sherman Street, each named after a literary giant—Alcott, Twain, Dickinson—Denver's Poet's Row. The increased height of the buildings made him feel claustrophobic.

The worst-case scenario invaded his mind. Handcuffs. Jail. Life behind bars.

The death cocktail.

Worse. They think he murdered a decorated police officer. Yes, Slager was a child of Africa, but there's no way Eli would even make it to death row.

Eli imagined himself falling, anticipating the concrete below.

They'll do to me what they think I did to Slager.

Sweat dripped down his beard as he struggled to catch his breath.

Eli was running.

(Twenty days to live)

THE BARBERSHOP

Liza walked; her mind raced.

That morning, during breakfast with Journey, they caught up on school and prepared for her spelling quiz. Liza loved these moments with her daughter.

Each day Liza noticed a little bit more of herself in Journey's expressions and mannerisms. The day before, Journey wrapped her hair in a scarf, put her hands on her hips, and sang a song to her stuffed animals.

Liza could also see a lot of her father in her too. Journey got his eyes and free spirit.

Jonathon Jones was older than Liza by enough to make her feel safe. What she didn't know was that he'd already settled on the life of a perpetual bachelor but had yet to hone his exit strategy or get a vasectomy. He had everything a woman wanted—good job, seemingly sweet personality, and dimples that he also handed down to Journey.

Journey hadn't seen him in three birthdays, and while Liza never spoke ill of him in front of her, she had given up asking to see him.

"Mommy, why are you sad?" Journey asked after spelling all the words on the quiz correctly.

"What do you mean?"

"I can tell you're sad because you didn't put any makeup on or wrap your hair."

"Little girl, you are too smart for your own good."

A few minutes later, in the car on the way to school, Journey continued her questions. "Is it Daddy or Papa?"

You can't protect her forever.

Liza spied her daughter in the rearview mirror. "Baby, it's Papa."

"Is he going to die?"

Liza pulled the car over and moved to the back seat.

"Baby, I don't know. I hope not. But I—"

You have to tell her.

"Remember how I had the big plan to go to court and confront that witness?"

"Yeah, Denzel! You were going to trick her with that hunk of a man!"

"What?"

"That's what you called him when you were talking to Grandma. You said that Denzel was a hunk of a man and that Eli was sexy as—"

"All right, little girl, you need to stop listening to grown folks' conversations."

"Yes, ma'am."

"OK, so you remember. Things didn't go well for us. The judge ruled against Papa."

"What does that mean?"

How do I say this?

"Does it mean they are going to kill him?"

Liza didn't know whether to answer that question with her head or her heart. After all these years of believing that there must be a way, that if she worked harder and smarter than anyone on either side of Langston's case, then he would be home in time for the next Fourth of July fireworks show at Elitch Gardens. But the judge's ruling had her mind spinning, and she wasn't sure if there was enough time to get the DNA tested. She decided to be honest.

"Baby, I don't know. They sure are trying to, so we need to get you down to see him this weekend. OK?"

"OK."

Liza moved back to the driver's seat.

"And Mommy?"

"Yeah, baby."

"I understand why you didn't put on any makeup."

After dropping Journey off at school, Liza stopped by the 7-Eleven, wrapped her hair, and did her makeup in the restroom.

She left her car in the parking lot and made her way down Welton Street. She was at the far end of Five Points and could see The Roz in the distance.

The fight in her was still strong; she was not going to lose her father. As long as there was time, she was going to keep trying to make a way out of no way.

Liza was on her way to The Shop, the place where Langston had cut hair and held court.

She'd loved it when he allowed her to tag along on Saturday mornings. The sound of black men laughing and jawing at each other made her want to be there every day. Even when they were loud and argued, she felt safe in their presence. Though it had been years since she'd been there, she remembered the floor plan. Four hair chairs on the left, along with a mirrored wall facing seven chairs on the right, the walls papered with *Jet* magazine beauties.

The Shop was the parliament of Five Points. There, decisions were cemented, wars averted, and, thanks to Langston, men became men.

Arriving at the candy-cane barber pole, she took a deep breath, opened the door, and stepped into her childhood sanctuary—now as a woman on a mission.

"Billie!" said old man Williams as he threw his hands in the air, clippers still buzzing, dancing with his eyes and feet.

The chairs were full, both sides. Those on the right rose in her presence, out of respect for Liza and in honor of Langston.

"Gentlemen, Daddy needs your help."

(Nineteen days to live)

THE DEATH CELL

Today was moving day.

You got this. One step at a time.

Langston sat on the edge of the concrete slab where he'd laid his head for as long as he'd been on death row. On his lap sat a half-full shoebox that would go to his family upon his execution. Inside were pictures of Elizabeth, Liza, and Journey; a collection of Nelson Mandela's prison letters; and Langston's toiletries.

An old Langston Hughes poem lingered in his mind, just out of reach of his memory. He searched for a word, a fragment of the elusive stanza. He hunted the prairie of his mind, rustling the underbrush until one word took flight like a pheasant bent on not becoming dinner.

"America."

One word was all he could remember.

The electronic sliding door in the corridor buzzed, announcing the arrival of his moving crew, shifting his mind away from the poet and back to the present. Langston could tell by the echo of their shoes that two were coming his way.

Play it cool.

Langston set his box aside, stood, and turned his back to the rectangular pass-through in the door.

When the guards unfolded the opening and stooped down to holler for him, they were startled to find him ready, hands behind his back, positioned for the cuffs and shackles.

Langston's neighbors watched his departure through their pass-throughs, their only connection to the world beyond their cell doors.

As Langston passed by, they assured him that each of them would be there for him and then in unison, like a military chant, "You will hear us!"

They were an odd family of misfits united by their common destination. Each knew that one day they all would be strapped to the table and put down like dogs to the cheers of a bloodthirsty country. They had resolved that the last thing each of them would hear would be the sound of support, so on the night of an execution, as midnight approached, they tapped on the pipes, and when the fateful hour arrived, they would all stomp three times and together proclaim, "We are with you!" It was a small way of letting the condemned and anyone else who was listening know that there was love among this odd-fellows band of brothers.

Langston nodded his gratitude to each one as he passed.

"Open D2," said one of the guards into the radio on his shoulder.

The heavy door slid open by a remote signal. Langston, flanked by his guard detail, took two steps into a small square room with two doors. He'd only heard rumors about this part of the prison; now he was gaining firsthand knowledge. In front of him was the entrance to the execution chamber. To his left was his new home, a six-by-six cell similar to, though slightly smaller than, the one he'd just left, with a concrete slab, sink, commode, and small TV in the corner.

"Here we are, Browny," said the guard on his right, making a tour guide motion with his arm. "Your new home."

Langston nodded with complete knowledge that here he would eat his last meal and receive his final prayers.

The guards unshackled him and closed the door behind them. Langston was surprised by their lack of taunts and jabs; they seemed to recognize for a moment that he was different from the others in demeanor and depth.

As Langston walked toward his bed, the news conference on the small screen snatched his attention. He couldn't believe his eyes as the camera showed a crowd standing outside his old barbershop with men—his old friends—holding signs that read "or ELSE!"

Standing front and center, leading the charge, was none other than his only offspring—Liza.

Langston sat down to watch his daughter shine.

Baby girl, what are you up to now?

Liza's head wrap stood tall, and her silver hoop earrings reflected the late morning sun. Langston was grateful for his old friends from the shop who were standing with her, providing their strength as Liza summoned hers.

When she and Journey visited that weekend, Liza would tell Langston that she had invited all of Denver's news outlets but only two showed, Channel 2 News, the smaller of the five local television stations, and *The Weekly Word*. "I don't know how they ended up there with their hotshot reporter, but having her was as good as having all the other print outlets combined, for what they lack in distribution they make up for in influence."

On the television, standing in the midst of many of Langston's old friends, Liza began to speak.

Show 'em what you got.

"Thank you for coming here today. While I hope the whole city will hear this, we are here to get the attention of one man and one man only—Governor Stash, we are here to put you on notice."

"RALLY FOR LANGSTON BROWN" crawled across the bottom of the screen.

"Governor, we are here because you are about to murder an innocent man." Liza paused. "Langston Brown is an innocent man."

She just won't give up.

"Time is of the essence. The clock is ticking." Langston noticed that she touched the tattoo with the fingertips of her left hand; her nail polish matched the blue-green of the water that buoyed the thirteen-hour clock. "We must act now. Let me be more specific: Governor Stash, *you* must act now."

Liza was staring directly into the sole camera present.

"You alone have the power. And I," she looked behind her, "*we* are here today to say loud and clear 'or else!'" She made a fist and pounded it on an imaginary podium.

"Governor, exercise your power, 'or else.'"

The men joined her in chorus.

"Now, you may think that you don't have to listen to us because those of us here in Five Points are small in number, and you can get elected without us. But hear me, if you ignore us, you will find yourself feeling the pressure. So I say it again, use your power, 'or else.'"

"Or else!" the men continued to shout each time she signaled, raising their signs as punctuation.

"We are here, and we are not going anywhere. Governor, you must act now," in unison, "or else!"

Baby girl, you are playing with fire.

Langston knew what she was threatening. If there was unrest in Five Points, then there would be unrest in Denver, the state's largest municipality. In the 1960s, the residents of Five Points joined in with the Watts and Detroit riots. Damage was done, but not to the degree of what occurred in the other cities. It wasn't that people in Five Points weren't angry; they were. But as of yet, they hadn't had a spark that flew into their own backyard. Most thought it was just a matter of time before Five Points led other cities into the streets.

"I know what you may be thinking," she began, seeming to speak to the larger population of Denver. "'You're Langston Brown's daughter. Of course you think your father is innocent.' You might even be thinking that Langston Brown has received due process, that he's exhausted all of his appeals and more. All of that is true," she conceded.

"But that doesn't matter, and the governor knows it. Stash, you know that Langston Brown did not get the same benefit of the doubt that that white cop got for the same crime. So, governor, we have two words for you—"

"Or else! Or else! Or else!"

When their voices died down, Liza raised the stakes. "Governor, we have one request. There's an easy way for you to clear this matter up once and for all."

She's going to make a great lawyer, the whole city can see it. That's my baby girl.

"Let me make our request clear: Test the DNA evidence in this case. Governor, all you have to do is subject it to the latest science, and you can prove the integrity of your administration with this one decision. Just say the word. Test the evidence in the Langston Brown case and show everyone once and for all that you have the right man and that the right man is going to die."

Liza concluded, "Governor, we demand that you test the evidence—"

Or else.

CLOSER

That night Eli and Liza talked for hours.

Their closing time ritual was something they both looked forward to.

After taking care of her daughter, keeping up with her final class in law school, and holding press conferences, Liza needed someone—needed Eli.

Eli, nowhere near admitting it to anyone, especially himself, had started to need Liza.

"They stood there with those signs like we were back in the day fighting the struggle. All we were missing were some leather jackets and black berets." She clapped her thin hands, with the fingers all pointing in the same direction.

Eli noticed how her fingernails matched her tattoo.

"I heard the commotion, and when I looked down the street, I saw the crowd and TV truck. I ran out the door without even locking up and couldn't believe my eyes when I saw you and the guys holding court. I joined in from the back, 'Or else, or else.'" Eli pumped his fist with the words.

"Why didn't you tell me what you were planning?"

"It all happened so fast. After I dropped Journey at school, the idea jumped like popcorn into my head and I went for it."

"I'm amazed at how it came together."

"You know why it came together so easily? My daddy, Langston Brown, trained them well and loved them even better. These men—our men—need a cause to stand up for, a reason to use their God-given strength."

As he listened, Eli had to admit that she was beautiful. Liza sat in her typical attire—jeans, boots, tank top, and head wrap, bright green this time. Liza was beautiful not in the fashion model sense but in the real-world way when a woman becomes herself.

"Today they found their reason." She raised her glass of Moscato. "To Langston Brown."

Tonight there was nothing between them.

Liza was in her usual seat. Eli, however, was not behind the bar; instead, he sat next to her. Liza leaned on her left arm, Eli on his right, facing each other.

Yet Eli was still guarded.

They were becoming friends. He didn't feel guilty, but he also recognized that love doesn't ask permission to bloom. Eli's heart belonged to Antoinette, but he knew that Liza's was a free agent.

Eli was worried.

Then there was the matter of Slager. What would Liza do if she discovered that he was the mysterious priest on Slager's balcony? The journals. What if she found out that he had new information about Langston's case that he was withholding from her? At this point, Eli felt that Liza didn't need to know. On the one hand, all he'd found was an odd riddle that may or may not be relevant to the case. If Eli said anything, she might overreact, and he could go to jail. On the other hand, if the riddle could save her father's life and he didn't tell her about it, the outcome could be equally disastrous.

Even with the questions and doubts swirling in the background, the warmth between them peaked as they finished a second bottle of wine.

Eli's heart continued to seek understanding of the moment. What was happening between them? Why did he hire her that day? Was it pure altruism, or was he, deep down, hoping for something more? Regret started to trickle into his heart as he sat there with Liza and not at the candlelit table with Antoinette.

Outside, the night sky already anticipated the morning sun; they had lamented and laughed until dawn.

Now, with nothing else to say, Liza's and Eli's eyes bounced between their empty glasses and each other's eyes and lips and hips.

Two people, wounded by the world and betrayed by love.

"What's next?" Eli asked.

"Well . . ."

"The press conference," Eli clarified. "Now that that's over, what's next?"

Eli's question snapped Liza back to the painful nightmare she'd lived for way too long.

"What's next?"

She picked up her handbag and stood, preparing to make her way toward the door.

"Next we tighten the noose on Governor Stash, until he begs us for his next breath."

SILENT PROTEST

Governor Stash and the First Lady drank their morning coffee together in the marble kitchen of the state-provided governor's mansion.

He sat, she stood. Both harbored concerns.

They still had their house in Five Points for show, but
they had decided long ago that their future was out here.

As far as Stash was concerned, they needed to prove that
integration was the future. He didn't march all those years
before to stay in Five Points. On their first date, he said, "I've
been through the worst; now I'm gonna benefit the most. I
sat in so I could move up."

Mrs. Stash, being younger, didn't quite get the whole sit-in
thing, but she loved the sound of moving up. When they married, the gossip writers proclaimed that "Denver's playboy mayor
found himself a trophy." When he asked her if she was bothered
by the perception, she replied, "I'm good, just as long as my playboy knows that his trophy requires a large mantel to sit upon."

Stash believed her and decided to run for governor.

This morning he could see that she was nervous, but he
waited for her to initiate. It didn't take long.

"What are you going to do?"

The Weekly Word sat on the counter between them. Liza's face glared at them from the cover.

"Today *The Weekly Word*, tomorrow the *Post* . . ."

"Relax, I'll take care of it," he said, hoping that she didn't sense that he too was concerned about the fragility of her future.

He knew that she'd already been eyeing life beyond the mansion. Some said that he was destined for Congress, others the Senate. One national pundit even hinted that he would be an interesting vice presidential pick for the right candidate seeking to diversify his base.

When Mrs. Stash heard that, she asked, "Ooh, is there a mini White House for the VP? Better not be too small."

Neither of them, as ambitious as they were, had the presidency on their radar. They saw what happened to Jesse Jackson and wanted none of that.

He envisioned more power, and she more prestige. Both imagined a luxurious life funded by the lavish speaking gigs that were in the governor's future.

But they knew that one political misstep would make all of that disappear.

"Trust me, I got this. We can ill afford a Willy Horton debacle. I remember what happened to Dukakis when they put that black-faced criminal on the cover of *Time* magazine; Dukakis was done once he was seen as soft on crime. There's no tellin' what they would do to this black face if I let another black face off the hook for something as heinous as the Mother's Day Massacre."

They both finished their coffee.

"So what's on the agenda today?" she asked.

Stash ran down an array of tasks that go along with actually governing. None near as glamorous as the mansion would infer.

The governor didn't ask what Mrs. Stash was doing, for he already knew that she could be found dining every afternoon in the trendy North Cherry Creek district. She and her friends would sit on display on one of the many bistro patios with their boutique shopping bags at their feet for all to envy.

With his wife's spending habits and their real house loaded up with a second mortgage, he could not afford to make a mistake. It wasn't easy to maintain a trophy.

"Well, Mr. Governor, I know you'll figure this one out," she said as she picked up their mugs and carried them to the sink.

He joined her and cuddled up behind her with his hands on her well-maintained waistline.

"Mrs. First Lady, what do you say we have dinner at seven and dessert around ten?"

"I like the sound of that, Mr. Governor. Where would you like me to make reservations?"

Before he could answer, he felt her stomach stiffen as she looked out the window.

Beyond the manicured lawn and flower beds thick with the state flower, past the driveway, and on the other side of the iron security fence stood a solitary black man.

He held a sign that read "or ELSE."

"Honey, trust me. I'll take care of this."

(Eighteen days to live)

LAST MEAL

The guard delivered the yellow cafeteria form with Langston's morning breakfast.

Langston was already awake. Life in the death cell was torture. The lights remained on throughout the night, and the guards checked on him every fifteen minutes. The irony of trying to make sure that people didn't kill themselves before they were executed. The constant opening of the door outside his cell, the shuffle of the guards' feet, and the anticipation of the stone-faced glare through the cell window were enough to make anyone want to die. Langston wondered if this was some CIA tactic, employed to wear the condemned down to the point that their execution seemed like a relief.

"Just let 'em know what you want. They'll cook almost anything."

"All these years you feed me slop for breakfast and dung for dinner, and now that you gonna kill me you want to know what I want?"

The guard huffed away.

Laid across the bowl of watery overcooked oatmeal was a yellow slip of paper that read

Last Meal Request

Drink:
Entrée:
Dessert:

Langston fumed at the idea that there was an actual form. "How many of us are they planning for?"

He spit on the paper, but his anger soon gave way to longing.

Last meal?

His mouth watered as he imagined the smell of collard greens simmering and pumpkin pie in the oven. Thanksgiving at the Brown house was a weeklong event. Elizabeth shopped the weekend before, prepped late into Wednesday evening, and woke up early to create the culinary masterpiece.

What do I want?

"Some crack mac 'n' cheese!"

Elizabeth's macaroni and cheese was so good that Langston often quipped that she was putting more than cheese in it.

Every year, when Langston headed out to prep the deep fryer for the turkey, Elizabeth would make him promise not to put them on the late-night news by burning the house down.

Drink?

"Colt 44 delivered by Billy D himself."

Langston's eyes closed as he remembered their last Thanksgiving meal. With the Cowboys on in the background, he joined hands with Elizabeth and Liza and blessed the food. Liza dreamed about Juilliard; Elizabeth watched as her family enjoyed her feast.

"Momma, you really put your foot in this," said Liza. They all laughed as they remembered when Liza was little and couldn't figure out why that was a good thing.

He could almost taste the sweet potato, hot with steam and so big that it required a separate plate as it sat split and mashed with two scoops of brown sugar crusting above and three slabs of butter on the top.

Langston's heart was full.

What do I want for my last meal?

"I want my family back."

Langston crumpled the form and threw it at the toilet. He missed, and it settled on the floor in the corner.

"Death," he was now speaking at the door to his cell, "you haunt and heckle, but I say you ain't got nothing to take from me that ain't already been stole."

Langston's mind then flashed back to a movie he and Elizabeth had seen about a slave castle in West Africa and a modern-day woman who was mystically transported back in time to experience the horrors firsthand.

She was captured, branded, and held in the female dungeon. At night they stripped her and delivered her to the captain's quarters.

He remembered how the film depicted his people in small underground holding rooms, crammed by the hundreds so tight there was no room to sit.

Her last meal?

Their food shoveled on top of them through the only source of light and fresh air high up on the wall. If they couldn't catch their meal as it fell, then they had to pick it up from the feces-covered floor.

Her door?

When the ships arrived, she was led out through the tall, wooden, iron-hinged door, never to see home again—the Door of No Return.

Langston felt like that woman. Except in the movie, she woke from her trance; he was stuck in his nightmare.

He turned and knelt. His left hand on the toilet seat steadied him as he fished for the yellow ball of paper behind the toilet.

"I stand with you, all of my people. We stand together."

He retrieved the small golf pencil from his food tray. Little did they know that he hadn't eaten since they put him in this holding cell. Every meal they delivered he'd flushed down the toilet as he fasted in anticipation of meeting his maker.

Langston thought about his innocent ancestors who were lost in the Middle Passage as they crossed the Atlantic. What would they have requested for their last meal before they jumped overboard into an ocean of certain death?

Their appetites and cravings would only be satisfied with one thing, and so, in solidarity, he knew what he wanted.

Langston unfolded the crumpled form and wrote his request: "I choose freedom, or ELSE."

KNOCK, KNOCK

Eli's prayer bracelet rubbed against the calluses on his thumb and forefinger as he lay on his cot.

Slager was on his mind.

He'd read through all of Slager's journals.

The responsibility of bearing the knowledge they contained overwhelmed him.

Eli believed Slager's writings held the key that would unlock not only Langston's cell but the cells of countless others as well. Slager told the truth, mostly under the guise of fiction and book ideas. At times he named names, included dates, and—Eli was convinced—recorded actual details of the crimes he committed in Five Points, first as a patrol officer and then as a detective.

He couldn't go to the police. They'd arrest him on the spot, for if he had the journals, then he was also the black priest who, in their minds, murdered Slager.

Eli had to figure something out, find another approach to sharing the truth.

He mulled over the riddle Slager had written on the same page as Langston's name. "Beneath the dormant stench of death it lies." What would he do if he decoded it? How would he tell Liza about it? What if he figured it out too late? How would he explain to Liza that he'd withheld the one thing that could have saved her father's life all because he was afraid that he'd end up on death row himself?

A knock on his front door echoed through his underground sanctuary.

The cops?

Eli's mind jumped.

They're here to take me away.

Eli surrendered to the fact that he was about to join Langston as he climbed the ladder and closed the hatch. Maybe they won't find the journals, he thought. Or perhaps it would be best for everyone if they did.

Again, a knock. This time sterner.

EVEN CLOSER

Liza turned to walk away, but then she heard the door open with purpose.

"I'm so sorry," she repeated twice before turning. "I shouldn't have."

Her eyes beheld a barely clothed Eli as he stood before her wearing only gray cotton workout shorts, revealing solid legs and a tight, toned upper body.

She tried not to react.

What do you expect when you summon a man out of bed in the middle of the night?

"I'm sorry, I should have just called in the morning, but I . . ."

She tried not to stare.

"I need to ask a favor."

Eli's face, then shoulders, sagged. She wasn't quite sure what to make of it.

"It's just that you left, and we didn't have our evening debrief."

Eli was now back on track with Antoinette.

"I'm sorry, I'll call in the morning."

As she turned to go, Eli spoke, "It's OK, come on in."

Inside, Liza still didn't know what to make of Eli's place.

"Please, sit down." He motioned to the table with two chairs. Eli took the chair with the orange scarf.

Liza noticed the two wineglasses on the table, the drying wax of the candle, and the smell of lavender.

Oh no! Someone else is here! What did you expect? But where?

"I'm so so sorry. You have company. I should have known there was—"

"I'm alone," Eli interrupted. "Relax. How can I help? You said you needed a favor."

Liza recalibrated.

"Two weeks. Eli, they're going to kill Daddy in two weeks!" She bit her lip, determined not to cry.

"I can't imagine. What do you need? Anything . . ."

He was kind as usual but distant.

"Time off. Can I have the next two weeks off? So I can try . . . so I can do all that I can?"

"Of course. I'd thought about asking but then thought you might need the money too. Or the distraction. Tell you what, business is good. Let's call it a paid leave of absence. I'm sure some of the others wouldn't mind picking up some overtime."

Her eyes teared up, so she bit her lip harder before replying. "Thank you."

He nodded. She looked at the two glasses.

Liza was genuinely confused. He answered the door dressed as if he had been sleeping.

But where's the bedroom? There's not even a couch in this room. There's only one door.

"Eli."

Liza looked around.

"I have to ask, what is this?"

No response.

Liza still couldn't gauge his mood, but she didn't sense anger.

You have to know.

"Eli, you know everything about me—how I fell in love with the wrong man, had Journey, and how he betrayed and abandoned us. You know about my dad and how desperate I was when I walked into The Roz that afternoon."

Still nothing.

"But while you know me, Eli, I know next to nothing about you outside of work. Please, tell me about you . . . about her . . ."

Liza sat, still and quiet. She was determined to let the silence do its work.

Eli's gut heaved, and his shoulders tightened. It was if a dam threatened to break.

He folded his arms, as if he was cold, hands wrapped around his elbows.

His eyes darted from her face to the glasses on the table and back again.

Liza waited.

"I can't survive."

His stomach and neck heaved together this time.

"Last time I almost . . . The Roz, I'd be dead if it wasn't for . . . I would have."

Eli fell silent.

Liza couldn't believe that he was talking and dared not say anything.

But if you don't, you're going to lose him.

Liza remembered something Langston used to tell her.

"Sometimes the only way to ward off a flood is to open a spigot," Liza said.

"Antoinette. That's her name."

He let go of his elbows and grabbed his shoulders.

"She's my everything."

Liza noted the present tense of the statement.

And then he started talking.

Eli told her how he met Antoinette and about their fairy-tale marriage.

"That's so beautiful. Please, tell me, what happened to her?"

She waited as Eli stared at the floor, clenching his jaw, but he kept going. He told her about the sickness and Antoinette's unbearable suffering.

"She's my world," Eli trailed off. Liza again took note of how he spoke of her in the present tense.

They sat in the stillness of his pain.

Liza then looked down.

She wasn't sure when it had happened, but they were holding hands across the table.

Liza felt grateful for the gift that Eli had just given her.

She also felt hopeful that perhaps, given enough time, they both could love again.

(Fourteen days to live)

MEETING OF THE MINDS

Governor Stash was feeling the pressure.

Everywhere he went, solitary black men stood silently with signs in hand.

Liza was using the governor's PR appearances as her own. Cameras went wherever he did, and so she did too. Liza's and Langston's men from the shop were relentless.

Signs reading "or ELSE" were the last things he saw when his chauffeured Suburban left the driveway of the governor's mansion and the first thing he saw at each corner of the state capitol building as he arrived at his office. Black men with signs greeted donors as they arrived for his uptown reelection fund-raisers, and when the *Denver Post* featured a picture of Governor Stash cutting the ribbon for a new school, one of Liza's men stood in the background with the sign in perfect focus and, in the foreground, Stash's face, clearly unnerved.

"Why do we publish my schedule ahead of time?" Stash asked rhetorically, though Mark Johnson, the mayor of Denver spoke anyway, as politicians are prone to do.

"Transparency."

They met, unscheduled and off the record, a few miles east of the city, just off Smith Road on a strip of land known as Emil-Lene's place. Due to a decades-old loophole, this swath of land had remained unincorporated by any municipality, surrounded by Denver and its suburbs but owned by none, governed by none, and taxed by no one but the federal government.

Emil-Lene's Steakhouse was the only structure on the land, and it had become the default place for surrounding government officials to meet on neutral territory.

Governor Stash and Mayor Johnson sat in the booth farthest from the door. Stash was grateful that he arrived before the mayor so he could sit where he preferred, with his back to the door to avoid being easily identified by those who entered. The booth looked older than the building, with its duct-taped cushions and yellow, faded linoleum tabletop. He thought of the stories this booth could tell of hand-shake deals, mistresses, misdemeanors, and likely even a few felonies.

"Neither of us can afford unrest coming from Five Points."

Though both were incumbents and ahead in their respective polls, neither needed additional headwinds to fight as election day approached. Stash knew it was only a matter of time before "or ELSE" T-shirts and hats would start to appear. At Langston's old shop, their most popular haircut quickly became the words *or ELSE* cut ear-to-ear around the back of the head.

"She's not going to let up," he said, talking about Liza. "Who knows what else she'll do over the next ten days. She'll do anything to try and stop Brown's execution."

Stash needed the mayor to cooperate with him. As governor, he had power over death row and the final say on all delays and pardons, but Liza's demand for DNA testing fell under the purview of the Denver Police Department. Only the mayor could give the thumbs up or down on that.

"We need to do something, we have to work together," Stash pressed.

"With all due respect, Governor, I'm not sure why we are meeting. I'm handling my business," said the mayor.

"Simply put, you let a renegade cop run unchecked and did nothing about it," Stash said.

"I did no such—" the mayor tried to respond.

"You did nothing about Slager," Stash said pointedly.

Stash knew that the mayor was clueless about the late detective's rampant abuse of power, so he unloaded all the dirty details about the city's beloved bad cop. He told Johnson about everything minus the information about the expired death drugs, which he kept to himself.

"All of that is on you. You were mayor during his rise, and if this comes out, you'll take the fall, not me," the mayor said.

Governor Stash continued, "Do you think he's the only one? You'll have to deal with the fallout from this for years."

"Yeah, but I'll be dealing with it from the mayoral office. You, on the other hand, will be sitting at home or in prison. Who knows, by then I might be living in your mansion, and you'll need me to pardon you."

Stash held up his hands in surrender. "I didn't come here to make threats but to ask for your help."

"Just get to the point."

"I need you to help me shift the narrative on this, just until we execute Brown."

The mayor went silent.

"In two days I'm going to announce a statewide task force to find Slager's murderer. We'll put the face of that priest everywhere and unite all the state's law enforcement entities—even the FBI is with us on this—so we can find the SOB who, in the dead of night, shoved our hero cop off his balcony to such a horrible death."

"But you've seen the sketch of that priest; it's generic at best," the mayor responded.

"Doesn't matter. Just release it." Stash raised his hands again and his voice softened, "Please, just release it, and when you do, announce that you have authorized the DNA testing of the evidence in Langston's case."

"Go on."

"So in two days I'll announce the task force, then you slow play this thing for another three days and reveal the sketch along with the DNA announcement."

"But what happens when the DNA results are released? Are you so sure you have the right guy?"

Stash was glad that the mayor seemed open to his proposal.

"Doesn't matter. Let me deal with that, but I can assure you, you'll have clean hands."

Johnson, not seeing any catch, continued, "And?"

The number of times the booths of Emil-Lene's had heard that question. What will you do for me? Where's the quid pro quo?

Stash was prepared.

"And I will throw a joint fund-raiser for us, and you take sixty percent."

The mayor didn't even acknowledge it.

"Come on, man, you know my connections. That'll cover half your campaign. What more do you want?"

"Two fund-raisers. Seventy percent," Mayor Johnson responded.

Governor Stash stood as if someone had just pulled him up by the scruff of his neck and turned to walk away. "Lunch is on you."

They both knew they had a deal.

(Ten days to live)

DON'T BELIEVE THE HYPE

"We did it!" Liza shouted as she swung open the screen door to the small but serviceable home where she'd grown up.

She made her way through the living room, past the sofa of her youth, to find her mother.

"Mom, where are you? We did it!"

Elizabeth stood at the kitchen window, looking out into the backyard.

"Did you see it? The mayor's announcement?"

Three days before, Governor Stash announced a statewide task force to find Slager's killer, and today Mayor Johnson released the sketch of the priest. Liza had tuned in like everybody else to see the reveal of the city's most wanted man.

"Ladies and gentlemen of the press, we believe there is a cop killer on the loose, and we need your help. Thank you for helping us get the word out."

Johnson spoke from behind a podium emblazoned with the city's official seal. The state and U.S. flags were in the background, and the chief of police and a few other officials stood in a rough semicircle around him. Prominently placed directly to the mayor's right was a sheet-covered easel.

He continued speaking, "But before we unveil the sketch, let me make a lesser—but by no means unimportant—announcement."

Liza couldn't believe the unnecessary drama. The television camera focused on the sheet-covered easel next to the mayor. Everyone wanted to see the sketch, and the mayor decided to make an announcement?

"We are committed to justice for all, and to that end I've charged our chief of police with ensuring that DNA testing is conducted for all the death row cases that fall within our jurisdiction, beginning with Langston Brown.

"We will also employ this new technology in all future prosecutions. However, given the gravity of death row cases and our desire for the public to have full confidence in our city's system of justice, I have asked our chief of police for these special reviews."

Eventually, after further DNA-related comments and various nods of agreement and support from the other individuals on the platform, the mayor unveiled the sketch of the priest. Liza had forgotten about the unveiling and immediately grabbed her keys and shot out the door of her apartment to celebrate the DNA testing news with her mother.

Her excitement had only increased during the five-minute drive to her childhood home. "Mom, did you hear? They're going to test the DNA! We did it!"

Elizabeth was still looking out the window.

"I'm so proud of all the guys down at the shop. They put the pressure on, and we got to them." Liza was revved up. "I know the window for testing is tight, but they can get preliminary results back in just a couple of days, which means when the news is out that Daddy is not a match, then Stash will have no choice but to delay the execution, and then," still not noticing that Elizabeth was not looking at her, "we are on our way to a full pardon. Mom, Daddy's coming home!"

Elizabeth finally turned and faced Liza. Only then did her lack of excitement come to Liza's attention.

"Mom, what's wrong? Don't you—"

"Honey, you done good, but it's over."

"What? No, don't you see, this is what we've been working for all these years. Our big break, this is it . . . the answer to all your prayers."

"Listen to me, Billie." Elizabeth was resolute. "You have to prepare yourself."

"Mom, why aren't you happy? Don't you understand that—"

"Get yourself ready. They ain't gonna let your daddy go. They ain't gonna let that black man off no matter what no science says."

Liza stood, shocked, but before she could continue to make her case, Elizabeth turned away again.

"Baby, your daddy is as good as dead."

(Five days to live)

THE SKETCH

Eli didn't know what to feel, whether he should be relieved or worried.

The sketch consumed the headlines of all the news outlets with barely a mention of the DNA announcement.

Eli was underground and on the phone.

"Freddie, tell me you guys are watching this DNA thing. Don't trust 'em. Something's up. Tell me you are on it."

"Of course we are, but it's going to be a few days before we can get anything out. Remember, we're a weekly publication. But, yeah, we're on it."

"A few days? They're going to kill Langston in a few days. You have to do something."

"Like I said, we're on it. But what about you? I'm assuming you've seen the sketch. Are you OK?" Fredricka asked.

"Well, I think every black man in Denver should be worried."

Mayor Johnson was right: the drawing was generic at best.

"It could be none of us, or it could be all of us."

Eli remembered how Sister Francis tried to explain to him that the children of Europe have a hard time noticing the differences among the children of Africa.

That's why the sketch doesn't resemble me?

Eli reasoned that the priest's collar must have distracted them and that they too shared the inability to truly see someone of the darker nation.

I guess we all do look alike.

"Eli, did you hear me?"

"I'm sorry, what?"

"I was asking if you're concerned or not by the sketch."

"Freddie, you tell me, should I be?"

"Well, while I don't think it looks exactly like you, there is one thing they got right—"

Eli interrupted, "Yeah, I noticed that too. I'm on it."

They spoke a few more minutes before hanging up.

Eli then unpackaged a new set of tweezers and began the process of reshaping and reducing the most distinguishing thing about the face God had given him—his eyebrows. They were loud and thick, like silky smooth black caterpillars. After several minutes of removing individual hairs, he compared what he saw in the mirror to the sketch on the front page of the *Denver Post.*

With a few more plucks, he was satisfied that he'd blend in with the sons of Africa who called Five Points home.

Eli then grabbed a sweatshirt as he headed out the door.

"Hoodie on high, head down low," he said to himself.

He hoped he'd done enough.

(Four days to live)

MISSING IN ACTION

Stan served in the depths of the Denver Police Department overseeing the evidence room. For almost four decades, he'd logged, stored, and retrieved every piece of evidence collected in every case. At one time, the evidence room was located beneath the courthouse at the City and County Building, but after a bond approval, Stan now had his own, medium-size two-story warehouse three blocks to the west. Nondescript so as not to attract any attention.

When he left the house that morning, he remarked to his wife of thirty-three years that he'd "probably get the call today." Stan, however, didn't expect that it would come from the police chief himself.

"Stan the Man! How are ya this morning?"

"Good, sir," he replied, with the formality that matched the actual status of their relationship.

"Well, I suspect you know why I'm calling."

Stan was well aware of the mayor's DNA testing announcement of the previous day.

"I'm sending a guy to pick up the evidence from the Mother's Day Massacre so we can overnight it to the diagnostic lab in Chicago. We'll worry about the other cases later.

Actually, he's already on his way, so if you could round it up and have it ready, that would be great."

"Yes, sir."

"Now, you know what we need in the Brown case, right? We need the shirt, the red shirt."

"Yes, sir, I'll fetch it up right now."

"Thanks, Stan, you da—" Stan was already off the phone and headed for the database system.

Not that he needed to look anything up; he knew the evidence room like he knew his wife's moods.

With verified coordinates in his head, he hopped into the golf cart and sped to the far side of the warehouse.

"Row seventeen," as he rounded the corner.

"Station twenty, box number four," he said as he locked the brakes.

Stan opened the box and flipped through the plastic ziplock bags, "EVIDENCE" printed in red across each one.

"Nineteen . . . nineteen . . . nine—"

Nineteen was missing.

Stan felt his heart accelerate.

There's no way.

He knew that he would never return any evidence to the wrong spot in the collection, but—to be sure—he checked all five boxes in Langston's case, none of which contained evidence bag number nineteen with the red, blood-stained shirt inside.

He raced back to his office and jumped out of the golf cart upon arrival, this time without locking the brakes.

He raced through the evidence logbooks for any record of who might have checked out the one piece of evidence that could clear Langston's name.

"Ahh . . . whew . . . here we go . . . Brown . . . bag nineteen . . ."

Stan's knees almost buckled, for in the signature space meant to identify the chain of custody, he found written in small print: "Beneath the Dormant Stench of Death It Lies."

REWARD MONEY

The next day, Mayor Johnson found himself in Slager's old office, with the press, standing, sitting, and leaning, crammed into the small cramped space.

"You played me!" the mayor said just minutes before in the neighboring conference room. "You knew it wasn't there, and now my integrity is on the line."

"You didn't think you were getting something for nothing, did ya?" Stash jabbed back. "If you name a high price, then you better be ready to share the commensurate risk. You're runnin' with the big dogs now."

Two hours after the impromptu press conference in the late detective's office, the mayor's chief of staff relayed the behind-the-scenes details of the drama to Eli back at The Roz while ordering another drink.

"Make it a double this time, no rocks," he slurred.

Eli would have cut him off, but he needed the information the chief of staff was slowly revealing.

"My boss was livid. Especially when Stash said, 'Relax, Johnson, you're pot committed. Let's see this through. Remember, control the narrative. Never waste a crisis.'"

The man began talking when a television reporter started to introduce the replay of the press conference on the TV above the bar.

"I know, I was there. Watch this. See how my boss just lets Stash do all the talking?"

Even without the man's guidance, Eli would have noticed how uncomfortable Mayor Johnson looked standing next to the governor.

"Thank you all for coming on such short notice," said Stash. "We've gathered in the office of the late Detective Slager, for it was here that he worked tirelessly to keep our city safe. It only seems right that we come here to make this announcement."

"Look at him, the red lights are on and he doesn't want nothing to do with it. When was the last time you saw a politician not want to be in front of the cameras?" asked the mayor's chief of staff.

"Today, we put our money where our mouth is," Stash continued, still leading. "With the launch of the statewide task force, we are now coordinating all jurisdictions in the search for the murderer, Detective Slager's murderer. Thanks to my esteemed colleague Mayor Johnson, the sketch of the evil man who dared to masquerade as a man of the cloth is available for all to see."

The mayor attempted an affirmation of Stash's boldness with a slight nod of his head and a tightening of his face.

"We know you are out there, and we will find you." The governor was looking directly at one of the cameras. "You can't hide forever. To ensure your capture, we are now offering a $100,000 reward to anyone who comes forward with information that leads to your arrest and conviction, Mr. Cop Killer."

The press conference ended with no mention of the missing evidence or their commitment to DNA testing in Langston's case. No mention that in three days, Langston would die.

Eli put the check in front of the man so he could pay. "You stay put, I'll call you a cab."

"Thank youse, my brother."

Eli served a beer to one of his regulars at the other end of the bar.

"Eli, did you see that? One hun'n thousand dollars for that black priest."

Eli now wondered if he was safe among the children of Africa.

(Three days to live)

NOW I LAY ME DOWN TO SLEEP

Langston lay on his back, straps pulled tight, cutting off blood flow to his hands and feet. The view of the fluorescent lights embedded in the ceiling was familiar. He'd seen them the day before in what those on the block call "Your Death Rehearsal."

The idea behind the rehearsal was to add a sense of routine to the stress-filled moments of the actual execution. Not only did the guards run through their paces multiple times, but the warden included what he called "a gentle walk-through, to familiarize the death candidate with what is to come."

Today, however, was no gentle walk-through.

Saline solution flowed through the needle that pierced Langston's left arm. The only sensation from this injection was the slight coolness of the room-temperature liquid, but Langston's veins would soon sense the jolt of the mixture of expired drugs.

The guards' taunts of "fire in your veins" had him involuntarily gripping his numb fists in anticipation of the burn that would soon creep through his body. He vowed to himself that he would not scream.

Don't give'm any satisfaction.

Final activities and quiet communications swirled around him. The chaplain leaned close and whispered in his ear. The slow, steady tapping of his death row family echoed down the hall and reverberated into the chamber through the old iron pipes.

Langston raised his head and surveyed the three windows.

Behind the first stood the two volunteer executioners and the warden who double-checked the dial tone on the wall-mounted rotary phone, the direct line to and from the governor should Stash choose to exercise his pardon power.

There's no chance . . . that phone ain't ringing with good news today. This is it.

Behind the curtain of the second window sat the families of the four guards slain in the Mother's Day Massacre.

They don't hate you. They hate the idea of you.

In the third room sat two people, holding hands, one in tired acceptance of an outcome she had seen as inevitable many years before, one in disbelief—Elizabeth and Liza.

They love you.

Langston laid his head back down.

HOME

An hour before, the Browns shared their last time together as a family.

Even then, the handcuffs were left on, and Liza and Elizabeth took turns slipping under Langston's arms for an embrace, trying to make the most of their limited time.

"Elizabeth, I was privileged to be called your husband." She melted in his arms.

"Billie, your daddy is beyond proud. You've done everything you could. This is not your fault. Promise me that you'll move on with your life."

She shook her head; mascara smudged his orange jumper.

"Can we sit for a moment?" Langston asked.

Elizabeth and Liza sat on either side of him on his bed slab.

Langston reached into his waistband and produced two sealed envelopes.

"Liza, this first letter is for Journey. Please give it to her next month on her birthday. Just want her to know that I love her and am thinking of her."

"And this one is for Eli."

Liza's eyebrows arched.

"I see how you look at him and lean on him in the court-room. He's been good for you, and I just wanted to thank him for all he's done."

It was more than a thank-you note. Earlier that day, Langston wrote to the man he hoped would someday marry his daughter: "Eli, though we've not properly met due to my circumstances, I can tell you're a good man by how Billie speaks of you and how you've supported her in the court-room. Thank you. Please, take care of my daughter, and if love grows between the two of you, you have my blessing."

Langston, Elizabeth, and Liza joined hands.

Elizabeth prayed aloud for her husband, and when she finished, Langston said, "I have one final request."

"Anything, Daddy."

"Take me home."

Liza was unsure what he meant, but her mom nodded, "We will."

Liza turned to her for some clue.

"Ashes. He . . . *we* want our ashes spread on the shores of Africa. We want to go home, together."

Langston waited a moment. He knew Liza was still in denial over what was happening.

"Will you?"

"Yes, Daddy. I will make sure you both make it home together."

AMERICA

Through the window, he saw the warden hang up the phone. Langston read his lips, "Go ahead." The governor had given the green light.

This is it.

The hands on the clock joined each other in pointing to the twelve, and, at once, three loud stomps from his surrogate family shook the room.

You are not alone.

The guard nearest to Langston looked down at him. "Mr. Brown, you'll now have the opportunity, should you choose, to speak your last words."

The gurney was elevated, and his body sagged as the straps held him in place. His hands and feet were blue.

The curtains opened in unison; Langston's eyes bounced between the two tear-filled rooms.

"Mr. Brown, you have been found guilty of four counts of murder in the first degree. We would like to give you the opportunity to make a statement before we proceed with your sentence."

Langston took his eyes off his wife and daughter and gave attention to the packed room visible in the middle window.

Their hatred was apparent, but he understood their pain. They had lost loved ones just as Liza and Elizabeth were about to.

"I know what you want," he began. "And I know what you need. You want to know why and you need to know that the man responsible for all your pain is paying for what he did. You deserve that. It's just that I can't give you either. I'm sorry."

Langston then turned to the right and spoke for the last time to his wife and daughter, "Elizabeth, I love you. I love you, Billie."

He then lay his head back in surrender.

The warden's voice broke the silence from the speaker above, "Proceed."

As the gurney was lowered back to its flat position, Langston's voice boomed, startling all who were present.

"America."

The poem that had lingered out of reach was, in this moment, reaching out for him.

"'Let America be America again. / Let it be the dream it used to be.'"

Langston was back in his mother's lap.

"'Let it be the pioneer on the plain / Seeking a home where he himself is free.'"

The gurney was now horizontal.

"'America never was America to me.'"

The staff hesitated, wondering if this should be considered part of his last words.

The warden interjected, "Proceed."

As choreographed, the two volunteers squeezed the syringes marked #1.

"'Let America be the dream the dreamers dreamed— / Let it be that great strong land of love . . .'"

He stopped.

The guards were right; fire coursed through his veins.

Langston forced a breath and continued with the words of his namesake,

"'Where never kings connive nor tyrants scheme / That any man be crushed by one above.'"

The sedative was taking effect, but Langston was determined, and with his final conscious breath, "'It never was America to me.'"

The protests in Five Points were far from silent that night.

PART IV

A certain
amount of nothing
in a dream deferred.
—Langston Hughes

ELI'S DESPAIR

Eli pressed the tip of the blade into his flesh.

It was an old Civil War relic that had been handed down in his family. Eli's grandfather liked it because it was northern in origin. He used to make up tales of how an escaped slave ran into a Union Army camp and enlisted on the spot. This was the sword that he was issued and used as he marched back south to fight for the liberation of his people.

But now, Eli hoped it would liberate him from his pain.

Eli pressed harder. His skin gave way.

This wasn't the first time he'd tried to kill himself.

Since Antoinette's passing, he'd thought about it many times, and on a few occasions, like today, he'd tried to muster the courage and do it. The last time was with a rope, but when he stepped off the chair, the noose broke, leaving him in a heap of despair.

"Baby, I need it to stop. I need you."

Eli had the sword's handle wedged in between Sartre and Camus, second shelf from the bottom of one of his many bookshelves. He figured that all he had to do was let go and let himself fall forward and gravity would take care of the rest.

He reasoned that if Slager could do it, then he could too. Eli knew that killing oneself doesn't come easily, but watching Slager step off the ledge like a child taking a plunge into a swimming pool gave him hope that he might be able to bypass his instinct for survival and let go, as Slager had. Eli wondered how many times Slager stood on his balcony rehearsing in his mind; many times, he must have stepped over the guardrail and leaned back. Eli was certain letting go as easily as Slager had required practice. He hoped that he would be a quick learner and that tonight would be his night of mastery.

For a while, The Roz was enough. The renovation kept him busy, but now that it was open, it only reminded him of what he'd lost. Eli and Antoinette sat across the street many times looking at the old abandoned building, dreaming about bringing it back to life, but now it lived, and Eli wanted to die.

At her funeral, the pastor told him, "In time, you will feel better. Yes," the pastor said, "you'll always miss her, but you will get through this."

But now Eli stood, sword angled up, aligned with his heart; his body leaned forward.

Eli's arms were the only thing keeping him alive as he released just enough tension in his elbows to feel the cold blade start its slide. Still sharp after all these years, the tip passed his skin and began to make its way into his abdomen, just below his rib cage.

Blood dripped.

The pain brought relief.

Eli steadied himself.

Out of habit, even at this moment, Eli scanned the volumes of books on the shelf, locating Viktor Frankl.

"My friend, you were right. Hope is the only thing that keeps us going."

Eli turned his attention back to the sword like a pilot going through his preflight checklist.

Everything was a go.

Deep breath.

OK, my man, you can do this.

Closed eyes.

Just let go.

Sweat mixed with his blood on the floor as the wound began to flow.

Just fall.

He remembered the promises he'd made to Antoinette, the night before she died.

"Baby, I can't do this. I've tried, but—"

Then, from upstairs, Eli heard a familiar knock on the door.

He covered himself as best he could and made the climb.

It was Liza.

This time, she was the one who saved him.

NOW WHAT?

They sat across the kitchen table, Eli preoccupied with the self-inflicted wound in his stomach.

He folded his arms and clutched his elbows to his sides as if he were cold. Beneath his zipped sweatshirt, a folded towel collected his pooling blood.

"How are you holding up?"

It had been three weeks since Langston's execution, and this was their first time seeing each other, though Eli had called and left a message of condolence.

"Eli, we're not doing well. I'm having a hard time holding things together. Can't get Mom to eat anything, hard enough to coax her out of bed. Journey keeps asking, 'Why?' and has nightmares almost every night because some kid thought it was funny to tell her that her grandpa had fire in his veins when they killed him. What the hell?"

"What about you? You can't be doing well."

"I'm not. I feel lost without Daddy. He was my rock. I still can't believe that he's actually gone. When I went to law school, I truly believed that I would figure things out, that it was just a matter of time, but then time ran out.

She was crying, but Eli was afraid that any movement toward a tissue would keep him from containing his blood. Plus, all he had was a roll of toilet paper, which was in his underground bathroom.

"I just feel so lost. I don't know what I'm going to do, and with Christmas coming, I want to keep things normal for Journey but don't feel much like celebrating."

"Holidays are the worst," Eli said. "They have a way of magnifying the pain and reminding you of everything you've lost."

For a moment, Eli wondered if that was the reason behind his despondence.

"Eli, I was wondering . . ." Liza paused and composed herself.

"So, if you haven't replaced me yet, I can come back," she offered. "The time off was helpful, but I need to get back into some sort of routine. I'm going crazy."

They spoke comfortably, not like two people who were strangers just a few months ago. They'd covered a lot of road in a short period of time.

"Of course, you can start as soon as you're ready."

"I can be there tonight, though I have to be honest; I don't know what I'm doing with my life."

I don't even want to live.

"I get that. I'm still not sure what I want to do with mine."

* * *

"True that. I'm far from ready to move on, but I need the money, need to take care of my daughter."

Eli released the pressure on his wound; he could feel the clotted blood gluing the terry cloth to his skin. Langston's letter ran through his mind. Liza had slid it underneath the door of The Roz about a week ago with a sticky note on the sealed envelope that read "From Daddy."

Eli wondered if she had read it.

Please, take care of my daughter, and if love grows between the two of you, you have my blessing.

If she had, she wasn't letting on.

If love grows between the two of you?

How could he take care of Liza when he didn't plan on being around?

Eli found Liza to be the strong kind of woman that he liked. Her beauty was matched only by the resilience that comes from meeting the challenges of life with courage and hope. Liza was a flower that stood in the aftermath of a hurricane.

Eli didn't wonder if he could love Liza; he had no doubt that he could. For him, though, he'd already been loved by a strong, beautiful daughter of Africa, and that love was enough—Antoinette was enough.

"I know I need to move on. Daddy wanted me to, but how can I? Did you see *The Weekly Word*'s exposé? Daddy didn't have a chance. They didn't even have the evidence to test for DNA."

Eli winced. Liza didn't notice.

"I'm convinced more than ever that this corruption goes all the way to the top. I don't know what else I can do, but I know what I can't do. I will not move on. The fight is not over, and I will not give up until the name Langston Brown is restored, vindicated. "

He nodded as he adjusted the towel and hoped that she wouldn't notice.

"All Daddy wanted was for his name to be cleared."

Eli considered taking Liza underground and showing her Slager's journals, but thought better of it. How would she react if she knew he was the priest from the balcony? Would she be angry if she discovered that he had hidden information from her? Would she ever speak to him again? Would she blindly go to the press and in the process get him arrested?

"So, are you OK with me working for you until I figure things out?" Liza relieved Eli of his thoughts. "I'd like to complete my degree and pass the bar, and then, hopefully, I'll know what to do next."

"Everybody's missed you, and I sure could use the help," he assured her.

When she left, Eli descended the ladder and sheathed the blood-crusted sword.

For the time being, he would work on Langston's dream—Liza's freedom—and then he would die.

DIAGNOSIS

That evening, The Roz welcomed Liza back with love, condolences, and respect for how she'd fought for Langston.

During a lull in the evening, Liza found Eli behind the bar.

"Eli, thank you for working with all of the uncertainty in my life and saving my job for me."

She caught a glimpse of herself in the mirror. During most of her fight for her father's life, she hadn't taken care of herself, either not thought about food or, as in the past couple of months, thought only about eating. She wasn't overweight, but she was finding it more difficult to get into her jeans.

I need to start running again.

There were a lot of things she wanted to start doing again—exercise and singing were at the top of her list. She was open to a relationship with Eli, though as soon as she thought about what she might like her life to be, all she could focus on was what she'd lost and how she might still prove Langston's innocence.

There has to be a way.

Liza, still looking in the mirror, focused on the tattoo of the thirteen-hour clock on her chest. She remembered when she had it done; it was the gift she gave herself when she got into law school. Even then she knew that time was against her, but she was convinced that her father would walk out of prison and be profiled on *60 Minutes* like other exonerees she had seen.

"Wasn't the same without you, though everybody thinks you might have a future in politics," said Eli.

"Say what?" Liza was now looking at Eli.

"Liza, people are drawn to you. We've all marveled at how you organized the men of Five Points into a cohesive unit that carried out a citywide campaign of intimidation that set Governor Stash back on his heels. If not politics, then community activism for sure."

"All I'm feelin' right now is that music. It's healing my soul."

The band was on point, and the crowd let them know it with accolades and—more importantly—tips.

Liza's mom, Elizabeth, even dropped by for a bit, saying she wanted to "hear some hip-hop with my be-bop." But Liza knew that Elizabeth was checking up on her.

When closing time arrived, Liza wasn't sure what to expect. Would their late night conversations continue now that they didn't have Langston's case to talk about?

After the last patron departed, she spotted two wine-glasses cradled upside down between the fingers of his left hand as Eli reached for a rosé with his right.

Thinking that he was on his way to meet with Antoinette, she was surprised by her level of disappointment. Now that her father was gone, other feelings were rising to the surface amid her grief. Before the execution, she knew that she was attracted to Eli, but now, she was feeling something else, something more substantial.

Liza wasn't jealous of Antoinette, quite the opposite; she was envious. She wanted to be loved with passion and fidelity, unlike her relationship with Journey's father, wherever he may be.

Liza knew that if anything were to happen, it would have to occur through their shared grief. There was no way to bypass their pain. She was convinced that if Eli had loved once, then he could love again.

So she leaned in.

"Will you tell me more about her? About Antoinette?"

He was still. She couldn't read his face.

"I know you're not over her; that's obvious to all of us." Liza didn't want to mess this up, so she reset. "I'm just saying that if you're up to talking more about Antoinette, I'm up to listening."

Eli turned and, to Liza's surprise, poured two glasses.

Seeing that Eli didn't know where to begin, Liza primed, "Tell me what happened. How did she die?"

Eli started talking.

"Life was good. We were good. Our life was good together."

Liza still couldn't place Eli's age. His beard was slightly gray, but his body was tighter than men her age, in their early thirties. She guessed late thirties, early forties at the most.

"My Antoinette was a dreamer, and after years of sacrifice and selflessness, we were about to soar."

Liza started to prompt, but Eli paused only long enough to take a drink.

"We were going to travel a bit, nothing exotic, just hit some of the national parks and then some extended time in New Orleans. After that, we didn't know how we could afford it, but we'd always dreamed of this place."

Eli motioned with his hands, his wineglass in one. "The Roz. What if we could have a place for our people to get away from it all, a place that felt like home?"

"Eli, what happened to her?"

"One day I came home from work, and as I walked in the door, she said that we needed to talk. I just figured that it had something to do with the bills or something, so I went upstairs and changed, and then we sat on the back porch like we always did."

Eli paused. Liza watched as he tilted his head back and clenched his jaw as men do when they don't want to cry.

"Antoinette, said, 'Eli, I'm sick, and the doctors don't know what to do. We don't have much time.'"

Eli breathed in through his nose and clenched his jaw again, this time swallowing.

"That was the beginning of the end."

Without warning, Eli stood up.

"Liza, thank you, but I can't. Not tonight. I need to go."

Liza watched as he opened the door and turned toward his home. He must have thought he was out of sight, but Liza saw him collapse partway to his place as he baptized the concrete with his tears.

At the bar, Liza sat in silent prayer.

PICTURE-IN-PICTURE

Eli did his best to get into Slager's head, and now he was concerned that he had succeeded.

It was 2 AM. His cot creaked beneath him as he sat bundled up head to toe in socks and sweats. The space heater tried its best to bring warmth, but the chill of fall was about to give way to the cold of winter.

As he reread Slager's journals, he tried to think like a good cop gone bad.

Slager thought of himself as a servant of the greater good—a black man who became a police officer for the benefit of those who resided in Five Points.

"I fulfilled my vow to serve and protect my community, my people," Slager had said that fateful night.

Slager's justification irked Eli.

"Those thugs were ruining everything. I did what I had to do to stop them."

But Eli understood.

When renovating The Roz, Eli fixed the front door three times and replaced the vast feature window once due to vandals. One of his most discouraging days was when he found the back door caved in and his tools stolen. The worst part was when the police caught the culprits—two black teens that Eli had hired to help with the renovations. It angered Eli that these two, from the community he was trying to help, were not helping him.

Hurting him while he was hurting.

As much as Slager troubled Eli, he understood how, after years as a beat cop, he turned bad.

Eli wondered how many times Slager had arrested a young black man who preyed upon the vulnerable? How many times did he comfort victims of crimes far worse than broken windows and stolen tools? Slager must have promised rape victims and families of the murdered that he would do all he could to give them justice.

Unfortunately, all he could led to crossing the line that led to injustice. All he could led to award ceremonies, his promotion to detective, and hero status in Five Points and beyond. Before he knew it, the daughters of Africa *and* Europe wanted to spend time in his company and his bed.

Eli shifted on the cot. It wasn't comfortable for sitting or sleeping. There wasn't much in his underground life that was comfortable, but that wasn't the goal. The books made him feel loved, and the heavy bag and lock on the hatch door were all about feeling safe and prepared, though with Slager gone, he wondered about the purpose of it all.

The pages of Slager's journals read like the confessions of a contrite and conflicted man.

Eli remembered what Slager asked him the night he took his own life.

"Do you think God forgives?"

Slager knew he was wrong, but—in the end—the cost of making things right had appreciated to a price far higher than he was willing to pay.

Slager made a successful life out of a self-dug pit. A good life that he was willing to do anything to protect. Including covering his misdeeds by manipulating Governor Stash into accelerating the executions of "those thugs."

Eli worried that he might be doing the same. Would his underground shrine of grief become a pit from which he couldn't escape? Would he even want to? If Liza confronted him the way he'd confronted Slager, how could he escape the consequences of what he had done and might do?

Tonight, as Eli attempted to make sense of Slager's stories, he focused on the treasure trove of details in the journals. There were names and specifics that pertained to other cases, other men on death row. What alarmed him the most was that Slager wrote buddy cop stories. The books he intended to publish were not of a lone detective solving crimes but of a hero cop and his sidekick. Chills rippled along Eli's spine as he entertained the possibility that Slager did not act alone, that there was another bad cop loose in Five Points. Eli knew he'd have to return to that terrible thought after he'd finished trying to solve the Langston riddle.

Eli felt isolated by his secret and inadequate in his pursuit. There was no one he could involve in this process without implicating himself or them. No one except Fredricka, but for the sake of his fidelity to Antoinette and his people, he needed to limit her involvement in his life. Period.

Eventually, he fell asleep without his workout.

*　*　*

The cut in his side reopened when he climbed out of his hole.

He wondered again if he and Slager were not all that different. If Liza hadn't saved him the day before, he would have been happy to have found his final resting place in his self-dug pit.

After he removed the old bandage, he tried using super glue to keep the wound from opening. He'd read somewhere that this was something that veterinarians did. Then Eli said goodbye to Antoinette and headed to The Roz for the morning's food delivery.

Behind the bar, he sipped his coffee and read the morning's headlines. With the news of the missing evidence reverberating throughout the city, it looked like Governor Stash was getting nervous. Mayor Johnson must have camped out at the mansion until they came up with a solution, another photo op in Slager's old office to announce nothing.

"Thank you all for coming," the governor began. "Your diligence is yielding numerous leads and, in the end, will help us bring a cop killer to justice."

Eli read the story below the picture that captured the meaningless moment.

"We're receiving tips by the hour and treating each one like it might be the break we've been waiting for."

Stash had the mayor retell the story of what happened to Detective Slager; the mayor used the opportunity to remind everyone of his own achievements.

And, once again, they highlighted the sketch of the dark-skinned priest.

"This is the man who masqueraded as a man of the cloth. This man is out there. We know you are watching, we are closing in on you. You might as well turn yourself in and save this city the headache of bringing you in like a dog."

Eli looked up from the newspaper and took a long glance out the window, searching for any extra parked cars with watching eyes.

He started to turn the page, but then he spotted something.

Above the fold was the picture of the governor and the mayor both holding the sketch while standing behind Slager's old desk.

Eli adjusted his reading glasses and leaned in.

There you are.

On the credenza behind the politicians sat a framed picture of Slager and his mother.

Beneath the dormant stench of death it lies.

Eli smiled, for now he knew where Slager had buried the missing DNA evidence.

The evidence that would have saved Langston's life.

The evidence that could still clear his name.

LAST DANCE

After telling Eli about her sickness, Antoinette lost her strength before the next full moon.

When she became unable to climb the stairs to their bedroom, he set up a twin bed for her in the living room, and that, unbeknownst to Eli, was where Antoinette would eventually speak her last words and breathe her final breath.

Eli camped out on the couch next to her.

At first, she was extra tired in the evenings and slept longer in the mornings, but Eli just thought it was because she worked hard or perhaps because she was depressed. He never suspected that his wife was terminally sick. That she was dying.

During the day, they sat hopelessly in the offices of every medical specialist they could find in the local yellow pages. At night, Eli agonized as Antoinette's pain increased.

One evening, during a lull in her pain, Eli lay down exhausted.

The ceiling fan whirred.

With each revolution, he found a new question for the God he wasn't sure existed. Father Myriel once told him, "God is not afraid of our questions, but we must be careful not to stand in judgment upon the Almighty."

In his youth, he didn't quite understand the distinction his mentor made. Yes, Eli had a difficult childhood, but children, fragile as they are, seem to thrive when tested. As a young man, Eli was as resilient as a toddler's plastic sippy cup. Yes, life left him orphaned and a ward of the local Catholic Charities, but he didn't know that life was supposed to be different.

So when Father Myriel tried to explain by saying, "There's a difference between questions and questioning," Eli didn't understand the difference until he lay helpless next to his dying wife.

That night, Eli toed the line and even crossed it a time or two.

Antoinette woke and, out of habit, reached for Eli. Her fingers found his face; her husband's silent tears moistened her fingertips.

"My man, we'll get through this."

He loved being her man.

"Trust me. You'll get through this."

Eli climbed into the bed next to her and held her as he had on their first night together.

The ceiling fan cooled.

Eli's tears wet both of their cheeks.

Antoinette started to hum. It was the song from their first dance as husband and wife.

"Dance with me," said Antoinette. "I'm not sure how much longer before I lose the strength to stand."

In the darkness, he found the turntable and set the record.

Eli helped her rise and held her up.

Etta began to sing.

Antoinette continued to hum.

She stood on his feet the way daughters stand on their fathers' feet when they're young.

For a few moments, they paused, swayed.

They kissed their last real kiss, as husband and wife.

* * *

It was late, but tonight Eli was not underground. Instead, he was far outside Five Points, walking.

Liza's questions had him cycling through his last, precious memories of Antoinette.

Then, in an instant, from every conceivable direction, the police; tires screeching, lights blinding, and guns pointed.

Eli raised his hands in surrender.

PROBABLE CAUSE

"Just lie there and shut up!"

Eli didn't feel as if he had a choice given that the burly man in blue had a knee in his back and cuffs sunk into his wrists.

"I said, shut up!" the heavy officer barked.

A pebble indented Eli's cheek, caught between the concrete and the bone beneath his skin.

Eli wasn't aware that he had said anything to warrant the second admonition to be quiet, but he was fine exercising his right to remain silent.

Eli was afraid because—unlike Langston—he had been at the scene of the crime. He was in Slager's home when the detective leaped. He was the black priest who stood on the balcony and passed the couple in the hallway.

But his fear was deeper, visceral. Father Myriel used to say, "There is a deep history between the children of Europe and the offspring of Africa when it comes to who gets to stop who and who ends up wearing the chains. This fear, over time, became an innate instinct causing the children of Africa to sometimes run from the police for the same reason that gazelles run from cheetahs. It's become a biological, evolutionary response."

When they first rolled up, Eli wanted to run, but his feet stayed planted. Now, with pebble pressing, he knew why. He counted at least five police cars and at least as many officers as there were front seats.

Where did they all come from?

"What are you doing out here so late?"

Thought I was supposed to shut up.

"Just walking," Eli said.

"What?"

"Just walking, trying to clear my head."

"Clear your head from what?"

Eli decided to tell the truth.

"Life. Just trying to figure out what to do next."

"But why here?"

Eli's face was on the sidewalk just outside the entrance to Denver Botanic Gardens. Antoinette had something of a green thumb and loved to peruse the variety of plants and flowers, both local and exotic, that lay behind the red brick walls. Though they never had children, Eli would take her out to brunch on Mother's Day followed by an afternoon stroll through the majestic acres. It wasn't his thing, but it was hers.

The picture of Slager and his mother that Eli spotted in the photograph of the governor's press conference was taken here, inside the botanical gardens.

Why am I here? I'm looking for a way in because I think this is where that crooked cop Slager stashed the missing evidence in the Langston Brown case.

Eli decided to lie.

"I don't know, just out walking."

"Yeah, right."

Eli initially assumed that they pounced on him because they'd solved the mystery and decided that this was the time to bring him in so they could parade him before the media in the morning with Governor Stash declaring a victory for the city now that they'd captured the cop-killing priest.

Now, however, he was getting the sense that maybe something else was going on. Outside of the police officer on his back, they weren't roughing him up. Eli imagined fists flying and boots stomping when he got arrested for the murder of Slager, their brother in blue.

Eli decided to test the waters.

"Officer, why'd you stop me?"

"You know, so just shut up and tell us where your car is."

Eli recognized the contradiction in commands but decided to comply with the command to be quiet and continued to exercise his rights.

Car? I don't even own a car.

Perhaps they weren't surveilling him as he'd suspected.

Another police vehicle arrived, this one unmarked. A uniformed officer exited, and given the way the others deferred to him, Eli concluded he was in charge.

"What do you want us to do, Sarge?" said the officer on Eli's back. "He says he's just out walking, but there's no way—"

"Cut 'em loose."

"But Sarge—"

"You heard me. Let 'em go."

What's going on?

The burly cop released his weight and loosened the cuffs.

Eli sprang to his feet, still feeling like he wanted to run, but the sergeant, with surprising humility, began to speak. "Sir, I apologize for any inconvenience we have caused you this evening. We had a report of a burglary in the area, and you happened to match the description of the person we were looking for."

What description might that be?

He wanted to confront them but figured silence was the better strategy.

"We've caught our guy, just a few blocks away, so, again, sorry for any inconvenience. Do you have any questions for me?"

Eli had a myriad of questions. First and foremost, what would have happened if they hadn't caught the other guy?

"No, officer. No questions. I know you are just doing your job. Thank you for your service." Eli's deference felt as instinctual as his desire to run.

"OK, well, you're free to go," said the sergeant.

Eli took note that the sergeant was directing him back to Five Points.

Eli wiped the pebble from his face and complied.

LADY DAY

Liza looked stunning.

It was Friday, which meant reservation night at The Roz.

Standing room only, because tonight Liza stood center stage.

A black, form-fitting dress revealed not only the clock tattoo on her chest but a beautiful flower and butterfly mosaic on her left shoulder and upper arm. All gave way and framed the name of her daughter, Journey, placed on the inside forearm with a path that led into the unknown.

The waitresses whispered about her hair. No one had seen Liza without her customary head wrap, but tonight, she shed her scarf; her updo was the talk of all the ladies.

Eli, knowing that Liza put her singing on hold to work on Langston's freedom, put Tyrone up to finding out if she could still hold a note.

"Pops, she's still got it in a new old school kind of way" was the report that came back.

When Eli asked what that meant, Tyrone said, "Just wait and see. She's like back in the day in a whole new way."

That didn't make sense either, but Eli—along with every-one else—was eager to find out why Tyrone was gushing with pure enthusiasm.

Liza hesitated as she stepped into the spotlight and approached the lone microphone. She stared at her feet as her presence hushed the crowd. When the band began to play, even the cooks stepped out of the kitchen.

Liza's time as Eli's manager wouldn't last forever. Once she found her bearings, he knew she'd move on to another job, though he hoped that this might give her a reason to come around on occasion, and tonight was part of his plan.

Tyrone nodded, and Liza began to sing.

One measure in and a patron said out loud what everyone was thinking, "My oh my."

The irony of Liza's nickname was not lost on Eli. Langs-ton and Elizabeth chose "Billie" for a reason, and now every-one was finding out why.

Eli leaned over to Liza's mother. "She's standing on the same stage as the original Lady Day and holding her own. Sure wish Langston could have seen this. His baby girl is singing at The Roz."

"Oh, he sees it. I know he's seeing this," said Elizabeth.

Liza held the room, and Eli hoped he could hold on to Liza.

She sang an old song by Sarah Vaughan about a woman waiting for love to come her way.

It was clear to Eli that she was hoping to hang on to him. Though Eli's heart wasn't ready for love, he had concluded that their futures were somehow connected.

Antoinette always used to tell him, "Things happen for a reason."

Eli trusted that Liza walked into The Roz "for a reason."

They both had loved and lost, and they both needed to move on.

"Maybe," Eli whispered to himself.

Not a man in the room could deny that there was something about the way she moved her shoulders and hips to the rhythm of the upright bass, not even Eli.

Eli contemplated how he might help Liza clear Langston's name while keeping the journals a secret.

He had a plan.

The band backed down as Liza's last note rang true. Even the drummer joined in the ovation.

"Thank you . . . thank you," Liza acknowledged as she glanced from the stage at Eli behind the bar.

They both knew that a new chapter had begun.

PERSISTENCE

"Freddie, you have to do something," Eli whispered with force across the table at Pete's Kitchen.

Waitresses squeezed their way past each other through the narrow walkway. The people in the booth across from them were close enough that Eli could smell the green chili on their breakfast burritos.

"You have a team of reporters chomping at the bit. Set them free," he whispered, now without the force.

"You're acting like we've done nothing!" Fredricka was not whispering. "We splashed it on the front page: 'Where's the DNA Evidence?'" She gestured with both hands. "We were the only ones in this town with that story, and now the whole city knows that something has gone awry. What else do you want?" Both of her hands now pointed at Eli.

"I'll give you that," Eli softened. "That story was good."

She raised an eyebrow.

"Really good," Eli adjusted. "And I'm sorry if I'm making it sound like you've done nothing. Not my intention . . . but what about the cocktail of death?"

Eli closed his eyes and tightened his jaw at the thought of fire flowing through Langston's veins.

"Freddie, we have to put an end to all of this before more people suffer—"

She started to interrupt.

"And you know that there have to be more Langstons. He wasn't the only dove on death row."

"We covered the expiration dates angle in the same piece as the missing DNA, but we don't have anything new . . . unless there's something more in those journals."

"It's just that Stash and Johnson keep producing more distractions. You need a follow-up story." Eli's hands were now pointing back to Fredricka.

"Speaking of follow-up, you've yet to follow through on what you promised." Now she was whispering with honey in her voice.

"Remember how you came over that one time? Eli, I know what you need."

"Freddie—"

"You need that Marvin Gaye kind of healing. I'm not asking for a lifetime commitment, just a commitment to spend life together, one night at a time."

Eli, in a moment of weakness, had found himself in Fredricka's arms, and she'd determined never to let him forget. It had happened in the aftermath of Antoinette's death, before he locked himself away from the outside world. He'd been vulnerable, and she was persistent—then and now.

"Freddie, that can't happen again."

"But you promised."

"Well, I'm struggling to keep a lot of promises right now." Fredricka pouted.

"I'm sorry. Can we just talk about a follow-up article? Please don't let things die with Langston and the turn of the news cycle.

"OK, I have the perfect follow-up." She picked her napkin up off her lap and tossed it on the table. "How's this for our next story, 'Fake Black Priest Found in Possession of Dead Cop's Property'?"

Now she was whispering with force.

Eli glanced at the smothered green chili burritos.

"Freddie, you wouldn't."

"Eli, *you* are the biggest news story this town has seen since the Mother's Day Massacre."

Eli knew she was right.

She leaned in. "Look, I'm not going to out you. I know you didn't push Slager off that balcony, but you have to help me. Instead of coming over to my place, how 'bout you let me come over and check out those journals for myself?"

"Freddie, look—"

"Eli, my hands are tied until you do something. Give me something solid to go on."

"You don't have anything else?" Eli asked.

This was the real reason why they were meeting. Eli needed to find out if there were any other options left before he did what he knew he needed to do.

"Nothing," she said.

"OK. I'll get you what you need, but promise me that when I do, you'll publish it."

She nodded, then added, "And I don't break my promises."

Eli didn't react.

"When and how?"

"I promise you, you'll know it when you see it."

"Tell me now, what is it?"

Eli decided to answer her questions with a question of his own.

"Ever looked beneath the stench of death?"

FLOWER OF DEATH

Denver is a divided city.

Like most places, the haves live in one part and the have-nots live out of sight of those whom they serve. In Denver, the have-nots live in Five Points—that's where the children of Africa purchased their homes and raised their children. In Denver, having and not having are less a matter of economics and more about the continent your ancestors came from before they arrived on the shores of America. In Denver, there are children of Europe who are struggling to make ends meet, but they don't have to live in Five Points, where the schools are underfunded and the water doesn't taste good.

In Five Points, the finest doctor resides next door to the man who shines his shoes. That is, until recently when some of the children of Africa decided to move out to the suburbs—Aurora, Montbello, and Green Valley Ranch—where their money said they could and should live. But on Sunday, the divisions are clear, as each nation worships in its own church, the children of Europe in theirs and the sons and daughters of Africa back in Five Points.

In Denver, there are only two things that bring those inside Five Points together with those outside—the Denver Broncos and, every ten years, Stinky.

The flower rarely blooms.

Once a decade, if you're lucky. Native to Sumatra, the titan arum sits idly the majority of its existence.

Its Latin name, Amorphophallus titanum, *translates as 'Giant Misshapen Penis."*

Eli laughed, disturbing the quiet of the central branch of the Denver Public Library.

He'd ventured outside Five Points, this time in daylight but still with his hoody on high and his head down low. He blended in with the majority of the men of Five Points given the cold temperatures that were now setting in.

Eli was still shaken from his encounter with the police the night before.

One of the first clues that pollination time is approaching is a growth spurt in which the plant can add as much as four feet in height in a matter of days, producing a large green scallion-like phallus.

Eli read from the marketing material that Denver Botanic Gardens released a few years back. The library archived everything.

Then the watch is on, for the flowering phase of this botanical giant is short-lived. Within twelve to forty-eight hours of bloom, the flower withers. It will be at least another decade before the cycle repeats.

Denver Botanic Gardens has one of these unusual plants on display. When it blooms, it's a citywide event. Everyone goes to see it, to smell it.

They've named it Stinker. For when the flower of the titan arum blooms, it smells, bad.

Eli never took Antoinette to see the flower in full bloom, one of his many regrets, because he despised crowds, and bloom time is crowd time at Denver Botanic Gardens.

It's a rite of passage, as the gardens stay open around the clock for some thirty thousand people to file through the greenhouse to experience the unbearable.

"Like dead rats," said one girl.

"Rotten fish," said her brother.

Eli turned next to an account in the *Denver Post*.

People proudly purchased overpriced T-shirts that proclaimed "I Smelled a Stinker."

The Corpse Flower, as it's also known, even got the city's coroner to stand in line and give his opinion.

"Yup, that's as noxious as anything I've ever encountered."

The putrid experience was livestreamed for the world to watch as people filed by the plant, some with handkerchiefs covering their noses; others became nauseated into the planter box that contained the flower; parents blushed at their children's fart and penis jokes; and almost everybody could be seen taking pictures in front of Stinker's four-foot-wide, rather beautiful, maroon, purple bloom.

Eli was interested in Stinker because Slager and his mother took the picture Eli spotted in the press conference photo in front of the plant.

Eli studied the material about the corpse-scented culprit because he was convinced that Slager's riddle led to Stinker. The evidence that could clear Langston's name and set Liza free was in Denver Botanic Gardens.

Eli couldn't conceive how Slager had done it, but somehow the detective must have hidden the missing evidence sometime between blooms of the pungent flower. If Stinky was the dormant stench of death, then Eli should be able to find the missing evidence beneath the flower of death.

PROMISES

Antoinette's breathing was like a flag blown in a fitful breeze. Her chest rose without rhythm or regularity.

Getting her to the doctor was now out of the question, and the ones who made house calls suggested hospice care. Eli was not going to let a stranger care for his wife in her last days. The truth became clear to Eli, as she lay on the bed in the living room, that here would be where he would lose the woman he loved.

If they had had children, they would have taken turns on the vigil, each staying home from school on different days, everyone camped out with her on the weekends. As such, a few close friends stopped by to say hello, only to realize that it was goodbye.

Eli never left.

When she was awake, she was lucid. These times allowed them to repeat "I love you" and say goodbye, again. But if Antoinette was awake, that meant the morphine had stopped working—her pain acute and intense.

Eli hated it when she fell asleep and despised it when she regained consciousness.

When she slept, he watched the ceiling fan. When she was awake, they tried to make the most of each moment, though, toward the end, it was clear that she was letting go. At her funeral, the preacher would say that she "began to care less for the stuff of earth as the stuff of heaven drew near."

That seemed about right.

When her eyelids were at rest, Eli's questions raged.

Why Antoinette? Why such horrible pain? How will I survive? Why can't the doctors figure this out? Where are you?

Eli wrestled with the stuff of heaven more than the stuff of earth, though neither made much sense to him.

He remembered when Father Myriel told him about the Eli of the Bible.

"There was this young boy, 'bout your age, who'd never heard the sound of God's voice. So one night, God started talkin', but the boy Samuel thought it was Eli, the priest, in the other room. Eventually, Eli told him, "When you hear that voice, it's God talkin' to ya, just say, 'Speak, Lord, for thy servant is listening.'"

Eli sat, heart full of questions, angry at the silence.

"Promise me . . ." Antoinette's whisper interrupted his battle with his mute foe.

He wiped the tears from his face, wondering if she'd sensed his anguish through the darkness.

"Yes, baby, what is it? Anything?"

She tried to sit up but couldn't. Eli propped her up on a pillow and felt the pain streak through her body.

"I need you to tell me two things," she said.

"What do you want to know?"

"He's been good to me, and I'm at peace. But I can't be OK knowing that you are in such turmoil."

Eli waited, not knowing how to understand those words with what he was witnessing.

"Tell me that you won't do this alone."

Eli didn't have many friends, and he was fine with that. Antoinette had always been enough for him. Everything he had and needed was in her.

Antoinette, however, knew that his well was dry.

"As I go home, you need to go home too."

"Netty, it's going to be OK. We'll get through this and when—"

"Listen to me. You need to let your soul go home."

Eli was now silent, so Antoinette mustered her strength in opposition. "Promise me. Tell me—"

"I hear you. I won't do this alone, I'll . . . go home," Eli said what she wanted to hear.

He knew what she was asking, but—given his struggle with things unseen—Eli knew that he'd promised too much.

"And the second promise . . ." Antoinette was determined. "You're not going to like this one, but I know you. After all these years, I know what you need."

Eli listened like someone hearing a song for the first time.

"Mr. Stone, my man, my husband. You have loved me well."

"You're easy to love," said Eli.

"Listen to me. You have loved me well because you need to love."

She paused for the reality of that statement to reach him, then continued. "Love is in your heart, and you're not happy unless you let it out. You need to love. My man, you are only happy when you are loving someone else."

Antoinette was stalwart, and she was not going to let her pain get in the way of helping her husband find his way through this ordeal.

"Eli, I bless you. I give you permission. You will survive this when you realize this truth about yourself: you must love."

"Promise me that you'll let yourself, love again."

Eli regretted nodding that night.

He knew what she needed to hear, and while she may have been correct in her assessment, Eli decided shortly after her death that he was never going to expose himself to that kind of pain again, that what he needed more than he needed to love was not to hurt.

That was their last conversation, for that night Antoinette died, leaving Eli alone.

Since that night, Eli had lived in denial of the truth spoken to him by the woman who knew him best—Eli needs to love.

INVISIBLE

Sister Francis was ecstatic to see Eli.

"It's been too long since you came to see me!" she fussed.

"You're looking well," she said as she made tea. "I hear The Roz is rocking.'"

Eli almost laughed.

"Whatchu snarking at? Can't an old woman stay hip and young. I know how to talk like the young folk!"

As the tea steeped, they caught up. Small talk and mostly who died and who was about to. Eventually, though, she opened the door for him to begin. "My dear one, what's on your mind? What's brought you home today?"

Eli told her everything, beginning with Liza and ending with Langston.

Sister Francis lamented the execution and prodded him about Liza.

Eli painted the picture of corruption from the governor's mansion to Slager and the cocktail of death.

"I remember Slager when he was just a boy like when I met you. He used to run up and down the street shoutin' 'Hi ho, Silver,' wearin' a white hat with his toy gun and holster. Always knew he was going to be a lawman."

Eli came clean, for he had never told her about how he used to eavesdrop on people's private moments with Father Myriel. He told her what he heard Slager confess the night Father Myriel was murdered.

"Oh my Lord," she said. Eli wasn't sure if she was responding to what Slager confessed or the fact that he listened in.

Eli told her what happened when he put on Father Myriel's collar and visited Slager's condo and the suicide.

At this point, she nodded. "I knew it was you. I saw the sketch."

"That's what I want to talk to you about."

Eli then told her about the night when the police stopped him and subsequently let him go.

"My son, I'm sorry."

"I've come to a conclusion about the children of Europe."

"Oh, really? Tell me about us," she said, half smiling.

"Sister, you've worked hard to understand the way things are, to be in but not of, and so I need you to tell me the truth about something."

"I'll shoot ya straight. My son, seriously, I'll tell you the truth."

You have to ask. It's the only way you'll know.

"Do they ever see us?" Eli asked

"What do you mean?"

"What all of this has led me to believe is that they never really see us. When they do, they don't. It's like we can't go anywhere and yet we can go everywhere. I mean, as I was leaving Slager's place, that couple saw me up close. We were face-to-face, but it seems to me that all they really saw was a son of Africa. They didn't see *me*. The sketch proves it. Outside of you, no one has recognized me, even though my face has been in every paper and all over the evening news. I'm still free. The cops saw me, and they didn't even know it was me. They haven't come to lock me up."

Eli threw his hands in the air.

"It's like when they see one of us, they see all of us.

"Which was bad news for Langston," she added.

"But it also seems that when they see all of us, they don't see any of us."

Eli then told Francis about the journals and the riddle and his theory about where Slager hid the evidence. He then returned to his question.

"Sister, here's what I need to know . . ."

Eli paused.

"I don't mean to offend you, but do *you* ever really see us?"

Now she paused.

"Sister, you promised to tell the truth."

"My son, to answer that question requires a lot of me, to admit a reality about my people and myself. I've worked hard to unlearn what America has taught me. But you've asked for the truth, and so the truth I will speak. No. We do not see you."

Eli sat back, slumped in his chair.

"I'm sorry."

"No, it's OK. It's what I wanted to know."

It was the answer Eli was looking for, because the testing of this truth was the only way he could see to find justice for Langston.

"Eli, how else can I help you? Is that all you needed?"

Eli thought about his last conversation with Antoinette and the promises.

"One more thing."

"Anything."

"I made a promise to Antoinette that I need you to help me keep."

"Don't you mean two promises?"

How does she know?

"Antoinette told me what she was going to ask you, about the vows she was going to ask you to take. My son, your wife has had us keeping watch over you in her stead. We didn't know if she was able to talk to you about her desires for your future before she died. But now I do."

Sister Francis rose from her seat and made her way to his side with the speed of a hurried snail.

"Tell me, how can I help?"

Promise me that you will let your soul go home.

"Will you—"

Before he could finish, she placed her hands on Eli's head and began to talk to God on his behalf.

Eli hoped that this counted as keeping his first promise.

CLOAKED

Denver Botanic Gardens was a sprawling oasis located just outside the downtown business district.

In the spring, the colors exploded like the Fourth of July. Reds, greens, purples, pinks, and blues leaped off acres of green canvas. Lovers strolled, teachers corralled their kindergarteners on field trips, and the seasoned citizens of the city made full use of their annual passes.

Though Eli had visited many times with Antoinette, he didn't recall ever seeing the corpse flower. He knew he'd never seen it in full bloom for he never would have stood in line to smell a putrid flower. He also didn't recall seeing it in its dormant phase. He could have, though, given that flowers weren't his thing and he would sleepwalk through most visits he and Antoinette made to the gardens.

He did, however, recall waiting in line at the front entrance with the children of Europe, and after paying the entry fee, the same people who made small talk with them outside asked them for directions and treated them like employees once they were inside.

Eli marveled at Antoinette's polite "I'm sorry, we don't work here, but perhaps the person over there might be of service."

That "person over there" was another child of Africa, wearing the standard employee uniform: brown boots, blue work pants, blue polo shirt with logo on the left, and a khaki baseball cap.

The same outfit Eli now wore as he bypassed the front entrance on York Street and made his way around the block to the back. He'd picked up the garments, minus the logo on the shirt, at the local Kmart. This morning Eli walked past the front entrance to the gardens and the spot where the police officer pressed his face on the concrete a few days ago.

He made his way around back and approached the massive back entrance gates that he'd scouted the night the police descended upon him. During the day, they were open wide. A delivery truck exited, a forklift moved a pallet of sod, and the children of Africa, all in the same uniform, went about their work.

Eli walked in.

Father Myriel once told him, "When you walk, walk like you know where you are going.'"

That's what Eli did.

He was a bit worried that his own might recognize him from The Roz, so he kept his cap pulled low past his forehead.

It was an unusually warm day for early December. Grounds crews set out to finish tucking in the flower beds for winter. Others followed with forklifts of poinsettias. Spotting a random rake, Eli grabbed it and slung it over his shoulder as he made his way past the wood-chip and manure piles and entered the vast expanse of gardens.

He set out across a large field cut with military precision, though the grass was light brown in color as fall prepared to give way to winter. Eli continued to make his way with steady purpose.

In the distance, he spied the mammoth three-story green-house that protected the gardens' tropical plants. That glass sanctuary was his destination.

The grass gave way to a cobblestone path with giraffe-high hedges on both sides. On his left, a crew trimmed, clipped, and bagged. As he passed, he traded his rake for one of their shovels.

No one noticed.

The large greenhouse now shaded him from the sun. Eli tugged on the brim of his cap and made his way to the employees' entrance.

Eli had an appointment with the flower of death.

THE DIRT

Sweat drenched Eli's makeshift uniform due to the humidity of the greenhouse. Island flowers and palm trees greeted him. To his immediate left sat a stack of white boxes housing the indoor hive of bees. The scouts took note of him but sounded no alarm.

Butterflies skipped silently above, their wings illuminated by the sun that shone through the myriad of car-size glass panels overhead.

Eli expected to find workers to whom he would have to explain his presence, but none were in sight.

The greenhouse was divided into four sections that each led to a central atrium. That was Eli's destination.

He spied a phone on the wall, and—after one last internal commitment to his cause—he picked up the receiver and dialed 911.

"Hello, what is the location of your emergency?"

"Denver Botanic Gardens, Boettcher Pavilion." That was the name of the inner atrium.

"And, sir, what is your emergency?"

"A crime is about to be uncovered."

"Excuse me, sir?"

No turning back!

"You heard me; a crime is about to be uncovered. Send the police now."

Eli hung up and grabbed the shovel.

The clock was ticking.

Now that he was on the inside, things were starting to feel familiar, though the atrium was larger than he remembered; the rows of plants and crusher-fine paths wound like a maze.

Eli, realizing the task at hand, began to run.

After a moment of panic, he saw it—the corpse flower. Eli stepped over the chain rope and looked up at the massive plant.

It sat in a five-foot-square wooden box, about three feet high, full of soil.

"Beneath the dormant stench of death it lies," Eli quoted out loud.

This is it.

He stepped in and began to dig.

The ground was soft, and the shovel sank with ease.

He discovered that the plant's roots took up only the center of the box, leaving a margin around the outside.

He wasn't quite sure what he was looking for, but when he hit the bottom of the box on one side, he moved to the next side.

Tossing each scoop of dirt outside the plant box, he trusted that someone would fill it in later and that the plant would survive, though that was the least of his worries.

The police are on their way. Faster.

Nothing on the third side of the box; he was on to the fourth.

Sweat soaked through his shirt and pants. The shovel once again hit bottom for the fourth time.

Nothing.

Surely the police had called ahead. The local observe and report security must be on its way too.

Hurry.

Eli's mind raced. What was he missing? Had he deluded himself into thinking that he'd outthought Slager? Did he really come all this way based on a hunch from a picture?

What now?

He slowed for an instant.

Beneath the dormant stench of death it lies.

Eli jumped out of the planter box like a scared rabbit and scooped a shovelful of dirt from the point where the planter box met the soil outside.

Beneath.

Eli dug like a rabid dog.

Beneath. Dig faster. Beneath . . .

The sweat that poured off his head and onto his face kept him from feeling the tears that streamed down his cheeks.

At Antoinette's graveside service, it was Eli who shoveled the first scoop of dirt onto her casket while those in attendance sang "Amazing Grace." Now, each shovelful of dirt only reminded him of what he'd buried with Antoinette. His grief was ever-present.

Everything. You were my everything.

His tears mixed with his sweat and muddied the dirt at his feet.

Why did you leave me?

Even in his pain, Eli made quick work of the hole next to the planter that contained the corpse flower. He was now on his hands and knees, scooping dirt out from under the box.

A cloud of dust rose from the dry soil, almost blinding him, but Eli was not deterred. He lay down, chest to the wooden box, right arm reaching, digging underneath.

We were just getting started.

Then Eli felt pressure pushing down through his shoulders, forcing his head into the hole, scraping his face on the rough wood of the planter box. His chest tightened. He struggled to breathe. A panic attack was about to render him incapable.

Not now.

His head smashed ear first into the wood. Blood began to run.

Why now?

Eli started to black out.

He decided to act before his foe dealt another blow and he lost consciousness. He stood up as fast as he could and swirled around.

"Wait, please wait."

He wasn't sure who he was talking to.

Oh, God no.

Eli's chest tightened even more.

Breathe.

His vision narrowed and darkness descended.

You've prepared for this. Breathe.

Eli raised his dirt-covered hands, formed them into fists, and took his familiar boxing stance.

Light on your toes.

Flashing through his mind like a low-grade slideshow was Father Myriel's dead body, eyes staring; Antoinette's coffin; and Slager falling.

Eli advanced.

Not this time.

Rage.

One time he told Sister Francis that he blamed himself for Father Myriel's death. She reminded him that he was only a boy, but he couldn't get past the fact that he froze out of fear, that he did nothing. "I didn't help him," he told her. "I didn't yell, scream, or even run for help. I cowered behind the cabinet as that man stomped the life out of him."

Eli moved forward, determined to take on all his demons with his bare hands. But with each step he took, they retreated.

"Come on. Let's do this. You've been doggin' me all my life."

Eli charged, head down, arms low, as if he hoped to wrap his arms around something.

"Come on."

Eli found the shovel, swung it like a baseball bat and let go. It crashed into the trunk of a palm.

Eli's fists were still raised as he considered his next move.

For a brief moment, Eli was underground with his heavy bag and stacks of books. He could almost hear Miles in the background.

He quoted Ralph Ellison.

I am an invisible man . . . I am a man of substance, of flesh, and bone, fiber and liquids . . . I am invisible, understand, simply because people refuse to see me.

Eli lowered his arms.

I am . . . we are, invisible.

He released his fists and spoke with a force fueled by the pain in his heart and the frustration of those he lived with in Five Points. He summoned a breath that would allow him to say what needed to be said, the only thing he knew to say.

"Be gone! Go away! Leave me alone! Be gone!"

Time was running out.

He wedged himself back into the hole, lying on his right side, lengthwise, with his chest and knees pressed against the wood. With his right arm, he fished underneath.

It has to be. Where is it?

Then he heard it, the crinkling sound of a plastic bag.

Eli strained to extend his arm and pinched the object between his middle and index fingers. Pulling it out of the darkness, Eli read through the dirt, written in red, "EVIDENCE #19—PROPERTY OF THE DENVER POLICE DEPARTMENT."

It was the missing shirt from the evidence room.

No time to celebrate.

Eli set the bag down and removed a folded piece of paper from his back pocket.

The note read, "To Mayor Johnson—The Missing DNA Evidence—Langston Brown."

Eli dared not delay.

As the police came in through the front entrance, Eli slipped out the back.

Unseen.

CAUGHT ON CAMERA

The 911 recording led the evening news, and everyone everywhere attempted to explain the unexplainable.

Who made the call and how did he know where the evidence was buried?

"'A crime is about to be uncovered'—then he uncovered it. Who is this guy?" One news anchor asked the question that was on all of Denver's mind.

The AM talk shows fielded a flood of callers, all with their own theories.

"He knew, but he didn't know," said one amateur sleuth, pointing out that the man made quite a mess digging around and under the corpse flower.

Visitors to the gardens that day were interviewed, but as Eli expected, none were able to identify the mysterious black man.

"Can you believe that the whole thing was caught on camera?" asked another caller.

Eli guessed right that the camera used to beam the blooming flower to the world was still broadcasting privately while the plant was dormant.

As Eli dug, calls came into Denver Botanic Gardens' front desk from research botanists around the world about the mad gardener and his crazy antics.

"That fool is going to kill our flower!" said one.

The whole time Eli searched for the missing evidence, he managed to keep his hat on and his head down. The camera never got a full shot of his face.

Eli watched with those at The Roz.

"What was up with his shadowboxing and his throwing of that shovel? Dude is crazy!"

"Maybe there's someone there, just out of sight," Eli said in his defense.

"No, man, it's a wide shot. Ain't no one there 'cept crazy man."

"I don't care who that man is, they should give him a medal. He found that evidence for Langston," another customer chimed in.

"Whatchu talkin', man, give him a medal? If he knew, then why didn't he save Langston's life earlier?"

When Eli decided to attempt his mission that day, he hoped there would be people watching somewhere who would be able to testify that he did, indeed, dig up the evidence. The last thing he wanted was for the story to circulate that the bag was planted there that day.

What Eli didn't count on was that there was a recording of the whole event. It wasn't just a livestream.

"Who knew that they archived the footage of a plant, doing nothing?" one caller wondered.

The witnesses along with the recorded footage meant that there was no doubt the evidence was not placed but merely uncovered by the mysterious black gardener. This also ensured that there would be no cover-up.

The governor and the mayor feigned happiness over the discovery and announced that the evidence would be tested "with as much haste as is scientifically possible."

The Weekly Word broke the story: Langston Brown was Innocent! Fredricka kept her promise.

The other media outlets followed suit: "Exonerated!" "We Killed an Innocent Man."

With calls for those responsible to be held accountable, the politicians did what politicians do.

Governor Stash called for a temporary stay of all executions until a full investigation of the matter could be conducted.

Mayor Johnson volunteered to "personally lead the special task force."

Elizabeth and Liza were invited to the state house and given an official apology.

Liza spoke with eloquence as to her father's character in the face of such extreme injustice and demanded that the politicians go beyond their apologies and entirely overturn the conviction, officially clearing his name once and for all.

A month later, a judge granted her request, and finally, Langston Brown's dream of a good name became a reality again.

As for the mysterious gardener, one reporter wrote, "He's the most wanted man in the city, second only to that priest."

LIZA'S DREAM

At The Roz, the grand opening crowds had settled into a regular core of customers who were there almost every week. These were supplemented by those who swung through for special occasions like birthdays and anniversaries. Business was going well enough that there was talk of opening earlier to catch the lunch crowd.

As far as Eli and Liza were concerned, both were trying to figure out life after everything.

Eli was settling into the life of a small-business owner, with its late nights and early mornings. It'd been a few weeks since the gardening incident, and he was looking over his shoulder less and less each day. Eli figured if they didn't know he was the priest, they probably weren't going to figure out that he was also the gardener.

Liza was spending more time with Journey and learning to live with the delayed satisfaction of knowing that all of the Mile High City now knows what she always knew—Langston Brown was an innocent man.

Today, Eli was straightening up behind the bar after the day's deliveries when Liza popped in.

"Figured I'd find you here."

For a moment, they both seemed to recognize that this was how it all began.

Liza sat down, taking her usual spot.

"Hey, thought I saw your tattoo guy in the neighborhood. Did he finish your latest work?"

"It's finished for now," said Eli.

"Can I see it?"

Eli hesitated.

"Please."

Eli lifted his shirt, revealing his abdomen, and on his right flank was a mourning dove perched on a branch of green leaves with five flowers; one red, four unfinished. In the distance, another dove took flight.

"Wow. That is absolutely gorgeous. Tell me about it."

"Well, the doves are a recognition of the truth in my life. Antoinette has spread her wings, and all I have is my broken heart to keep me company. Just trying to figure out what I should do with my wings."

"I can relate," Liza said.

Eli thought about how mourning doves are among the few animals that mate for life and how his life with Antoinette was far too short.

"So what's the significance of the unfinished flowers?"

"Well, five flowers represent the stages of grief."

"Oh, I remember those. Someone gave me a pamphlet on grief after Daddy died, and I think I've raced through all five stages a few times."

"For me, I've done the opposite of racing. Been stuck in the first stage of denial for a long time. But it feels like it's coming to an end. Trying to prepare myself for the next—"

"Anger."

"Yes, I'm afraid of that one. Terrified about how long it might last, but I definitely feel it coming."

Liza continued to focus on the mourning doves, and Eli tried to hide his scar, evidence of his inability to work through these stages in a healthy way.

"All right, enough about that. I'm guessing you didn't stop by to talk about my grief."

"Well, Eli, I was hoping we could chat."

"Sure, what's on your mind?"

"Eli, you've been good to me," she began with all seriousness. "And time has flown by since I first walked in here. You have been my rock."

Eli wasn't sure if this was a thank you or a proposal. His head desired neither, but his heart wasn't sure.

"Please hear me. I am beyond grateful."

"I'm grateful for you too. We've been through a lot in such a short time."

"Yes. And you know I love you, and I love this place, but I need to pursue my dream."

Eli's heart sank slightly. He started to align the barstools.

"Eli, it's going to be OK. I'll give you time to find someone to replace me, but there's something I have to do."

She touched him, and he stopped fussing with the stools.

"Liza, we've both known this was temporary. You walked in here looking for a drink, not a job." They both smiled.

"Well, remember what you told me." She pointed to the tattoo on his arm. "My future is in my past. I've decided not to run from all that I've had to learn out of necessity. I decided to accept a job with the innocence project. You are now looking at the new assistant director of Project Joseph."

She didn't pause.

"But I'll still be here. Tyrone has asked me to sing every Friday night, and I would love to. Singing is my passion. So I'll be here on Fridays, prime time, if you'll have me and if I'm good for business—"

Liza was already good for business in her management role, and she would be great for business as a regular onstage. Everyone loved her.

"But there are more!" Still not pausing and increasing her volume.

"Daddy was not the first, nor was he the last. There are more who have been screwed over by the system and are behind bars in America for crimes they did not commit. I'm going to find them."

Eli thought about Slager's journals.

Fear flooded as he remembered his secret. If she only knew how much he knew about Langston. Would she love him or hate him? Probably both.

Eli knew she was right. Slager's journals read like *The Confessions of Saint Augustine*, complete with times, dates, names, and details.

"I'm happy for you. Your father would be proud, and yes, you can sing here. If Tyrone hadn't offered, I would have."

"You're far from getting rid of me." Liza reached across the bar and touched his arm.

"And Liza," Eli was still thinking about the journals, "you're right. There are more, right here in Colorado. We're just getting started."

Eli wondered if she noticed that he'd included himself in that last sentence.

Before she could inquire about what he meant, he added, "I'm sorry, Liza, but there's somewhere I need to be."

Eli left as unexpectedly as Liza had arrived.

TOGETHER AT THE SAME TIME

As Eli departed through the front door, Liza read his mind. "Yup, I'll lock up."

"Thank you."

It was then that she realized something wasn't quite right with him. Yes, Eli was his usual supportive self, but when he smiled in celebration of her new direction in life, something felt forced.

He was sad.

Liza watched as Eli made his way down the sidewalk and crossed Welton Street.

He's wearing all black.

Liza ran to Eli's desk in the back room and found his planning calendar in the top drawer. Today read: Four Years.

She realized where he was going.

On the edge of Five Points lies the Riverside Cemetery, where the children of Africa lay their loved ones to rest, say their goodbyes, and return to express their regrets.

Liza went back to the bar and noticed a bottle of whiskey next to an item wrapped in a tablecloth. When she unfolded it, she discovered an old sword. She removed it from its sheath and admired it for its apparent age. Then she gasped. There was dried blood on the blade.

Mr. Stone. What were you thinking? Planning?

Liza gave him enough time to walk the five blocks to the front gate of the cemetery before she locked up and made her way in the same direction.

The sun was bright and the temperature unusually warm for this time of year. Most people she passed on the streets carried the coats they'd brought with them.

When she arrived, she spotted Eli in the distance within the cemetery.

Liza couldn't deny it any longer. She had fallen for him. There was a genuine love that had grown in her heart. She continued to follow, concealing herself in the shadows of the many clusters of evergreens.

What are you doing? What if he spots you?

Eli knelt at a headstone and wiped his cheek.

Today was the four-year memorial day of Antoinette's death.

He turned his back toward Antoinette's headstone and leaned back hard. His shoulders convulsed.

Liza was desperate to run to him, but she watched with homage and wondered if there would ever be a place for her—if there was even room for her—in Eli's heart. She believed there was, and that Eli felt the same too. She would go at his pace and grant him the space he needed to grieve—fully.

Mr. Stone, I'm willing to wait. I will be patient. Take your time, I will be here.

A movement caught her eye. In the distance, in another clump of trees, a blond woman.

What is she doing here? Did she follow me?

Fredricka watched Liza as Liza watched Eli.

AUTHOR'S NOTE

My wife's cancer forced me to face my greatest fear: life without her.

While Barbara was in treatment, people would often pull me aside to ask how I was doing. In my honest moments, I responded, "It doesn't matter," for I didn't feel I had the luxury of answering that question. I was trying to be supportive of my wife, present for our children, and on schedule with a publishing deadline—all while keeping up with work day after day. If I wasn't doing well, there was nothing I could do about it.

After three surgeries and twenty radiation treatments, thankfully and by God's grace, my wife was OK . . . but I was not.

There was a truth that her sickness forced me to face: in all likelihood, one of us is going to die before the other, leaving the survivor to deal with the pain—I could be the one to live longer. This truth became a suffocating visceral feeling that took up residence in my chest. Someday, something could take my beloved of more than two decades, leaving me to face a pain matched only by my love for her.

They Can't Take Your Name was my way of facing that reality, and then it turned into a crime novel!

Separating Fact From Fiction

I've lived my whole life in the Mile High City, and—like any author—I write what I know. Historically, Denver's black community found solace in a neighborhood known as Five Points where the historic Rossonian jazz club (The Roz) has sat empty for decades. For years, before gentrification set in, Five Points was a place that I would go to find respite from life outside our historic home. During these times, I'd often dream of restoring and reopening the legendary jazz club.

The Mother's Day Massacre was actually the Father's Day Bank Massacre that happened June 16, 1991, in downtown Denver in what was the United Bank building—what locals call "the cash register building." I borrowed the basic details from this unsolved crime in our city, including the fact that a former police officer was found not guilty in the same way described in the book. The crime and trial took place when I was in my early twenties, and I remember wondering if a black man would have been convicted under the same circumstances. This tragedy provided the basic framework for Langston's wrongful conviction.

In 2017, the state of Arkansas did, in fact, announce a plan to execute eight men over the course of eleven days. Such a mass execution season was unprecedented in the United States, and—as one would hope—many people rose in opposition. One of the reasons given for the rush was that the state's supply of the drugs used for lethal injections ("the death cocktail") had already or were about to expire.

Writing Wrongful Convictions

Unfortunately, wrongful convictions are all too real in our justice system. As I write, almost 2,500 men and women have been exonerated, totaling more than 21,000 years lost. Conservative estimates are that only 1–2 percent of all convictions are of innocent people. That's an impressive success rate, and it can be comforting to think that our criminal justice system incarcerates the correct person 98–99 percent of the time. However, this is not good news if you are among the 1–2 percent. Think about what that means in actual numbers. There are approximately 2.5 million people incarcerated in the United States. Conservatively, then, there are *thousands* of innocent people doing time for crimes they did not commit.

Have we executed an innocent person in the United States? I am not aware of a verifiable case of a wrongful execution. However, with the history of vigilante justice and lynchings in the United States and the sheer numbers of wrongful convictions in the modern era, it's reasonable to suspect it has happened. Having Langston, an innocent, meet his end unjustly was my way of trying to help us come to grips with this reality.

Our criminal justice system in the United States is broken. Reform—transformation—is needed to address mass incarceration and the fact that the largest mental health facilities in this country can be found in our jails and prisons.

What can you and I do about wrongful convictions? First, we should understand the well-documented anatomy of a wrongful conviction. We know the root causes that lead to convicting the innocent:

- False and contaminated confessions (innocent people pleading guilty)
- Eyewitness misidentifications (especially cross-racial misidentification)
- Flawed forensics and junk science (false or misleading experts)

- Jailhouse informants (trial by liar)
- Plea deals
- Incompetent counsel and/or inept lawyering
- Unscrupulous law enforcement professionals
- Corrupt evidence
- Shoddy investigative practices
- Lack of DNA testing
- Racial bias

Some of these causes must be addressed at the level of those in charge—police, district attorneys, and judges. But because our system is ultimately a very human system in which we are judged by a jury of our peers, we as citizens must learn to spot these root causes when we are called upon to cast judgment on someone's life.

Only a few of these root causes made their way into the story line of *They Can't Take Your Name*, which means you'll be seeing more of Eli and Liza as they fight what I believe to be *the greatest injustice in our justice system*—wrongful convictions.

Read a Book, Right a Wrong

You've already made a difference just by purchasing this book (and future books in this series). I have donated a share of my advance and am committed to giving a portion of all future proceeds to one of my favorite innocence projects, The Korey Wise Innocence Project at the University of Colorado. The average cost to free an innocent person is enormous, and my hope is that this series of books will raise enough money that we might actually be able to say that together we had a part in somebody's freedom.

Please visit my website (RobertJusticeBooks.com) for more information about my *Read a Book, Right a Wrong* initiative.

Langston Hughes, Ralph Ellison, and All That Jazz

Jazz is more than music; it's a way of seeing and interacting with the history of America. This is why I love the work of Langston Hughes and Ralph Ellison. When Hughes wrote his poem "Harlem: A Dream Deferred," he was doing jazz. He was not the first of the jazz poets, but he is definitely the most notable. These poets began by including references to music and musicians in their prose. Then they quickly embarked on applying what they saw the musicians doing on the stage and translated it into their verse. Making use of the elements of jazz, they gave birth to a new way of doing poetry—poetry in jazz. Read Langston Hughes and you find syncopation, improvisation, and call-and-response, especially as he interacts with the great American novelist Ralph Ellison.

Ellison was a trumpeter and lifelong lover of jazz. He not only asserted that all of American life is "jazz shaped"; he sought to demonstrate it when he wrote the great American novel *Invisible Man*. Ellison, a longtime jazz critic, moved from writing about jazz to writing in jazz. This is most evident in *Invisible Man*, in which he responds to the poetic call of his friend Langston: What happens to a dream deferred?

He hints at this in the prologue to his novel when the main character seeks to light his underground darkness by illuminating it with 1,369 light bulbs. The number is a coded tribute to the year 1936—the year Ellison moved to New York City during the Harlem Renaissance and met Hughes.

Ellison's work is a jazzlike response to Hughes's call: What happens to the American Dream when it is deferred for a group of people? (The answer, by the end of *Invisible Man*, is a resounding "It explodes!")

They Can't Take Your Name is my feeble attempt to join the Hughes-Ellison Ensemble. Eli's underground abode is a nod to Ellison's *Invisible Man*, and naming our innocent man Langston and including Hughes's poetry throughout this novel was my way of adding my voice to the conversation that they began about race in America.

ACKNOWLEDGMENTS AND THANK-YOUS

To my Father, who art in heaven, hallowed be thy name.

To my children—because of you, my cup overflows.

To Andrew—you've always been more than an agent, a true friend indeed.

To all my beta readers (Barbara, Jeff, David, Janella, Ten, Chris, Heather, Mihret)—your feedback was invaluable.

To Jevon Bolden and Shana Murph—your early editorial advice was pure gold.

To Progress Coworking—Joe and Biff, thank you for your kindness and generosity.

To the team at Crooked Lane Books—Thank you for all you did, seen and unseen, to bring this book into existence. Terri Bischoff, your editorial skills and encouragement along the way were invaluable. Thank you for believing in this book.

To the Crime Writers of Color group and all the listeners to the Crime Writers of Color podcast—I'm so grateful for who we are and what we represent.

And finally, to my bride, Barbara Anntoinette—you will always be my inspiration.

It has been said "Write something that may change your life . . . and when you're done writing the story, no matter what else happens, you've changed your life." I hope that those who read this novel are—at a bare minimum—entertained and perhaps enlightened in some way. In my most grandiose moments I dream of the end of the death penalty, for as Bryan Stevenson has so eloquently written, "The question is not do people deserve to die for the crimes they commit but rather do we deserve to kill." With our track record of arresting and convicting innocent people, we have long forfeited any right we had to take another's life. All of that said, regardless of the actual difference this book will make in the broader world, I'm certain that writing *They Can't Take Your Name* did, in fact, change my life, and for that I'm grateful.

Oh yeah, Denver is also home to two rare blooming corpse flowers named Stinky and Little Stinker.

Robert Justice
Micah 6:8